THE
GAME
OF WIZARDS

Psyche, Science, and Symbol
in the Occult

by

CHARLES PONCÉ

PENGUIN BOOKS

Penguin Books Ltd, Harmondsworth,
Middlesex, England
Penguin Books Inc, 7110 Ambassador Road,
Baltimore, Maryland 21207, U.S.A.
Penguin Books Australia Ltd, Ringwood,
Victoria, Australia
Penguin Books Canada Ltd,
41 Steelcase Road West, Markham, Ontario, Canada

First published 1975

Library of Congress Catalog Card Number: 73-90932

Printed in the United States of America

Typography by Martin Connell

To Dwight and Barbara
for their love and friendship
and
to Jabir,
that another door may be opened

Acknowledgments

GRATEFUL ACKNOWLEDGMENT is made for permission to use copyrighted material from the following.

"Akkadian Myths and Epics," translated by E. A. Speiser, in *Ancient Near Eastern Texts Relating to the Old Testament*, edited by James B. Pritchard, 3rd edition, with Supplement. Copyright © 1969 by Princeton University Press. Reprinted by permission of Princeton University Press.

"Transformations of Science in Our Age," by Max Knoll, in *Papers from the Eranos Yearbooks*, edited by Joseph Campbell, Bollingen Series XXX, Vol. III: *Man and Time*, translated by Ralph Manheim. Copyright © 1957 by the Bollingen Foundation. Reprinted by permission of Princeton University Press and Routledge & Kegan Paul Ltd.

"Hypothesis of Environmental Timing of the Clock," by Frank A. Brown, Jr., in *The Biological Clock: Two Views*, by Frank A. Brown, Jr., J. Woodland Hastings, and John D. Palmer. Reprinted by permission of Academic Press, Inc., and Frank A. Brown, Jr.

The Five Books of M. Manilius, translated by "T.C." Reprinted by permission of the American Federation of Astrologers.

Special thanks to Burton Sharpe for the photographs in Chapter 5 and for his informative discussions on Ptolemaic astronomy and to Samuel Bercholz, who understands.

Contents

Acknowledgments 7

Introduction 11

1. The Nightmare of Astrology 19

2. A Universe of Chance 75

3. The Structure of God 117

4. A Metaphysical Melting Pot 148

5. The Chemical Illusion 167

6. The Future Is Mind 204

Appendix A 220

Appendix B 229

Appendix C 236

Introduction

WHATEVER ONE may have to say about them, there is the inescapable fact that the occult sciences, some as ancient as Babylonia, have persisted. Civilization has on a thousand occasions attempted to shake itself loose of them to no avail—they continue to enchant, enrapture, possess, and enrage the sensible portion of man's psyche to this day. Even more disconcerting is the fact that in the midst of the twentieth-century Western world, that culture which prides itself on having achieved the most traditional and empirically based form of consciousness ever known to man, there is as much an involvement with the occult as ever before.

Most moderns tend to ignore these sciences, finding among their devotees an abnormally childish concern with the future bordering on paranoia. But there are a number of questions rarely asked: Why, if we can rationally dismiss these systems out of hand, do they remain? Why have people sometimes been willing to sacrifice their reputations and social standing to support the claims of such systems? To come close to an understanding of the phenomena, further questions must be asked: What psychological, metaphysical, or philosophic realities do these systems purport to reveal that so engage us? What is it about the nature of the psyche that is willing to support the existence of such systems? And even more importantly, What is it about the nature of the psyche that causes it to produce such systems?

Our dictionaries tell us that the term "occult" is derived from the Latin *occultus,* the past participle of *occulere,* "to cover over." In its original sense it simply referred to something that was hidden from sight, secret, or unknown. In the twentieth century the term has come to designate a particular body of inquiry or learning that proposes the existence of another dimension tangential to reality, one invariably defined as the motivating principle of the universe and therefore superior to empirical reality. The empiricist, operating from the premise that what is "real" is immediately discernible and scientifically measurable, dismisses the so-called phenomena of the occultist's universe as the product of chance or pure imagination. It follows that any theory proposing the existence of a dimension or quality of experience that is not available to direct and controlled observation is often scoffed at by the scientific community.

Our first objective will be to point out that certain branches of psychology also claim the existence of a dimension of reality upon which the conscious portions of our psyches are dependent, a dimension that is also inaccessible to direct observation and whose operations are not measurable by presently available scientific instruments. Most will recognize this dimension as the unconscious and will understand that its definition fits that given to the term "occult." All of which suggests that what was occult, i.e., "hidden," in these earlier sciences were the operations of the unconscious portions of the psyche. The suggestion here is a simple one: If we cannot accept these occult sciences as legitimate inquiries into the nature of being residing at the threshold of our senses, we must still accept the reality of the unconscious impulses that created them and seek their purpose. If nowhere else, it is here that we shall discover their value.

Also included here is the idea that the occult sciences have a value over and above that traditionally ascribed them, a value far more relevant than even that given them by occultists. It will be suggested that they are actually systems that place us in diréct contact with the unconscious. What the occult sciences speak of are certain regions of psychological awareness that we are only now beginning to perceive, aspects of mind as foreign to us today as the theory of the unconscious would have been to fourteenth-century man.

Some of the evidence to be presented, drawn from modern scientific studies, will suggest that we are affected by forces having their origin beyond the perimeter of the natural world, and may indicate the existence of subtle and as yet undefined receptors in our bodies that respond to these cosmic influences. Taken one step further, it may be said that it is their structure in part that is revealed to us in the symbolic systems displayed in the occult sciences. I say in part, for it is also contended that beneath these subtle or primary receptors there lies an organizing principle or archetype of order that is at base totally independent of the biologic or somatic operations of our bodies. As we shall attempt to show in the first chapter, although the operation and function of this ordering principle is sometimes confused with the physiochemical operations of our biology, it is an independent system whose nature is primarily psychological. In the presentation of the structural forms displayed at the heart of each of the occult sciences we shall see that it is the unconscious projection of this ordering principle, ultimately expressed in terms of number, pattern, and symbol, that gives shape to an occult philosophy they all share in common.

In pursuing these assertions, it will be necessary to dwell from time to time upon the philosophic background of certain seminal ideas contained in each occult science. This approach is important because each occult principle to be examined has its origin in philosophic speculation and not, as is so often thought, in magical or occult perambulations.

The occult sciences chosen for our investigation are those which have gained the greatest prominence in history—astrology, the *I Ching*, Kabbalism, the tarot, and alchemy. Of these, three are essentially divinatory in construction and use. The other two, Kabbalism and alchemy, are actually spiritual disciplines that incorporate certain elements of other occult systems. With the exception of the *I Ching*, an Oriental system, all of the arts discussed constitute the mainstream of Western occultism.

Take a look round, then, and see that none of the uninitiated are listening. Now by the uninitiated I mean the people who believe in nothing but what they can grasp in their hands, and who will not allow that action or generation or anything invisible can have real existence.

—Plato, *Theaetetus*

THE GAME OF WIZARDS

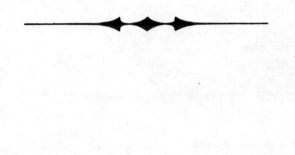

1

The Nightmare of Astrology

> The Consciousness of each of us is evolution looking at itself and reflecting upon itself.
>
> —Teilhard de Chardin

IT is only fitting that a work of this type begin with one of the most popular and least understood of the occult arts, astrology. From the time of the early Chaldeans to the present it has held man in total fascination. That an art that claims to be able to predict the nature of one's personality, the manner in which one will conduct oneself in the world or fail to, could actually survive modern man's empirical approach to reality is unthinkable, but it is so. There has been no civilization in the past that has not reserved a royal place for its astrologers at one time or another. But because of its seemingly outlandish claims, astrology has won star billing on the skeptic's list of man's foolishness. A brief outline of the philosophic background that led to astrology as a mode of perceiving man and the cosmos will start us off on this journey into the zodiacal universe.

Astronomy, and therefore astrology, came into being in Babylonia with the compilation of the first star catalogs and tables of planetary movements around 1800 B.C.

While the Babylonians were mathematicians of such caliber as to astonish twentieth-century experts with their achievements, they never attempted to discover the cause of the phenomena they so accurately recorded. Alexander the Great's conquest of the Babylonian cities in 331 B.C. resulted in a small and fragmented portion of these records falling into Greek hands. Further discussion of astrology in the West hinges on these Greek thinkers who gave to ancient astronomy a philosophic dimension whose end is still not known.

Astrology in the West

It might be said that whereas the Babylonians created a mythology out of their science, the Greeks produced a science out of their mythology. The early Greeks, the Ionians, had passed through the enchantment of mythological inscapes and were quickly turning to the observation of the cosmos as a piece of history to be discovered. Thus they first turned to two questions: What is the prime substance of the universe? and What, exactly, is the "schematic" of the universe? The first to come forward with an answer was Thales of Miletus (c. 636–c. 546 B.C.).

The Babylonians had thought of the universe as a closed, containing system surrounding the earth like a box, atop which sat the dome of heaven. Beneath that, resting on water and surrounded by oceans, was the earth. Thales' cosmology was conspicuously similar: The earth was a flat disk floating upon the water. Scholars today agree that he was more than likely indebted to Near Eastern thought for this view, since quite apart from the Babylonian cosmology, the Egyptians also believed the earth to be a flat, rimmed dish floating upon the water under a watery sky.

Thales' student, Anaximander of Miletus (c. 611–c. 547 B.C.), later offered a radically different view. He professed the world to be cylindrical in shape, three times as wide as it was deep, and floating freely in space. Surrounding it was a series of tubular wheels containing fire. Each wheel bore a hole through which the light of the contained fire shone. When one looked up at the heavens, at bodies of mass that were later known to be planets, what was seen was actually nothing more than these holes, the fixed stars being but the result of smaller holes in a large backdrop.

Shortly afterward a younger contemporary, Anaximenes of Miletus, revived the flat-earth thesis, also attributing this flat quality to all of the heavenly bodies. Imitating Anaximander's idea, his earth and planets were supported by air instead of water. This air, however, was not the simple element man breathed, but pneuma, an animating breath of life that coursed throughout the universe. In addition to this innovative stroke, Anaximenes also suggested that the result of heaven was a crystalline substance to which the stars were affixed like nails.

Pythagoras (c. 582–c. 507 B.C.) was the first to displace the earth from the center of the universe, placing there in its stead a central fire around which the earth and the other planets, sun included, turned. But the importance of Pythagorean cosmology lies in another quarter, in the theory of divine numbers. First Pythagoras realized that it is the *length* of a string producing a musical note that determines its pitch. Then, altering the lengths of the strings on a lyre, he found that the concordant intervals in the musical scale could be expressed in terms of simple numerical ratios. He then applied this concept to the cosmos, imagining a huge lyre with curved strings to represent a model of the universe. The distances between the planets were a function of his musical intervals.

> The Pythagoreans said that the bodies in the planetary system revolve around the centre at distances related by mathematical proportions. Some revolve more quickly, others more slowly. The slower ones emit deeper sounds as they move, and the quicker ones higher sounds. These sounds depend on the ratios of the distances, which are so proportioned that the combined effect is harmonious.[1]

From this cosmology arose the idea of the harmony of the spheres, in which for the first time the operations of the universe are symmetrical. The planets are spherical, their movements circular, and the universe containing them spherical as well.

The next cosmologist of interest to us, Anaxagoras (c. 500–c. 428 B.C.), contributed little in the way of either mathematical or mechanical theories. In fact, he believed in the flat-earth-supported-by-air theories. Nonetheless his proposal that the machinery of the universe had been activated by a universal mind, the nous, was to affect the whole of cosmologic and religious thought for several centuries. While the pnuema of Anaximenes

---

[1] Alexander of Aphrodisias (A.D. 3), quoted in Stephen Toulmin and June Goodfield, *The Fabric of the Heavens* (New York: Harper & Row, 1961), pp. 72–73.

was considered to be simply originating stuff without consciousness, the nous encompassed a new and exciting aspect in that it was seen as the very air man breathed as well. The nous of Anaxagoras was bolder in that it put forth the picture of an all-pervading mind:

> And Nous set in order all things that were to be, and all things that were and are now and that will be, and this revolution in which now revolve the stars and the sun and the moon and the air and the aether which are separated off. And the revolution itself caused the separating off, and the dense is separated off from the rare, the warm from the cold, the bright from the dark, and the dry from the moist. And there are many portions in many things, But no thing is altogether separated off from anything else except Nous. And all Nous is alike, but the greater and the smaller; but nothing else is like anything else, but each single thing is and was most manifestly those things of which there are most in it.[2]

This was a significant moment in the history of philosophic speculation and one that would in time affect the theories of astrology as well. Prior to the emergence of the Ionian philosophers the workings of the universe, the phenomena of nature, even the peculiarities of human nature, had always been explained in terms of divine and spiritual operations. With Thales we saw the first scientific attempt to perceive the universe as an amalgamation of impersonal, natural forces.

In a sense the development of astrology as a psycho-

---

[2] Anaxagoras, quoted in Frederick Copleston, S. J., *A History of Philosophy* (New York: Image Books/Doubleday, 1962), Vol. I, Part 1, pp. 86–87.

logical tool, an art by which the operations of the soul could be not only recorded but daily observed, begins with Socrates. Nowhere are we told that he had any concern with the astronomy of his time, but the concerns of later astrology are so similar in intent to his theories that it is difficult not to find some relationship. Socrates was the first of the great philosophers to turn from the observation of nature to the observation of man—specifically the soul of man. Up until his appearance there would be a considerable amount of cosmologic speculation, practically all of it mechanistic in scope. The pre-Socratics were to become obsessed with the discovery of the "prime matter" and the "original cause" to the point where they would become oblivious of man and his relation to both the cosmos and society. All they contrived to explain was how things came to be. Socrates would prompt the search for the soul.

Anaxagoras, therefore, plants an important seed with his theory of a universal mind. The suggestion that mind preceded the world would inevitably raise the question of the difference between this universal mind and the mind of man: the difference between the macrocosm and the microcosm with which astrology concerns itself.

Plato (c. 427–c. 347 B.C.), great in stature in so many other respects, has little personal impact in the history of cosmologic speculation. The detailed cosmology of the *Timaeus* is reduced to a thumbnail sketch in *The Republic*, where Socrates tells us that the universe may be likened to a series of whorls having the shape of a set of bowls. There are eight of them, we are told, set one within the other, their rims forming a level plane:

The circle forming the rim of the first and outer-most whorl (Fixed Stars) is the broadest: next in breadth is the sixth (Venus); then the fourth (Mars); then the eighth (Moon); then the seventh (Sun); then the fifth (Mercury); then the third (Jupiter); and the second (Saturn) is narrowest of all.[3]

Where Pythagoras for the first time created fixed intervals between the planets, Plato first suggested that the planets move at different but constant speeds:

the eighth (Moon) moved most swiftly; second in speed and all moving together, the seventh, sixth, and fifth (Sun, Venus, Mercury); next in speed moved the fourth (Mars) with what appeared to them to be a counter-revolution; next the third (Jupiter), and slowest of all the second (Saturn).[4]

It was obviously the authority of Plato's genius and nothing else that gave philosophic worth to the Pythagorean thesis that the planets moved in perfect circles. His insistence on this one point caused the whole of scientific thought to become obsessed with this fiction for the next two thousand years.

Aristotle (384–322 B.C.) kept the earth in the center of the system, but following the hint of Anaximander, placed around it nine transparent, concentric crystalline spheres. The outermost sphere, which was stationary but responsible for the movement of the inner spheres, was God. Then, in diminishing order, came the stars, Saturn,

---

[3] Plato, *The Republic*, trans. by Francis MacDonald Cornford (London and New York: Oxford University Press, 1971), pp. 353–354.

[4] *Ibid.*, p. 354.

Jupiter, Mars, the sun, Venus, Mercury, and the moon. Everything within the sphere of the moon, the sublunar region, was subject to the blemishes associated with change. In this system of the concentric movement of the planets, a major problem remained unsolved: If the planets moved as Aristotle and others proposed, their distances would remain constant, while to the observer on earth they appear to approach and recede in their motions. This problem was to defy solution for another five hundred years, until the appearance of Ptolemy.

Claudius Ptolemy was born at Ptolemais in Egypt around A.D. 100. During the seventy-eight years of his life it is believed he wrote fifteen works on science. Today some are regarded as spurious. Of these works two were to become the classics of astronomy until the seventeenth century: *The Almagest,* or *Syntaxis Mathematica,* in thirteen books, and the *Tetrabiblos,* the latter to this day referred to by astrologers.

Ptolemy wholeheartedly accepted the theory that the planets must describe perfect circles to the point where he practically issued it into law: "We believe that the goal that the astronomer ought to aim at is the following: to show that the phenomena of the heavens are reproduced by circular, uniform motions." [5]

In addition to proving this he also set out to solve the problem that had been a thorn in the metaphysical side of every cosmologist since the time of the Babylonians: the retrograde or apparent backward movement of certain planets. And solve it he did, to the satisfaction of thinkers for the next several centuries. His solution, too lengthy and complicated to present here,[6] involved re-

[5] Ptolemy, *The Almagest,* iii, 2.

leasing the planets from their ensnarement within the crystalline spheres of Aristotle's system and fixing them to wheels moving at different ratios to one another. The mechanical operations of these wheels, forty in all by the time the system was completed, is a lesson in imagination and must have cost many an astronomer and astrologer many a sleepless night. Whatever the modern mind might think of Ptolemy's geocentric system, the fact remains that for all practical purposes it worked. Columbus and Magellan plotted their courses by it.

Because the whole of classical astrology developed around the Ptolemaic system, it remains the basis for the greater portion of objections against this occult art.

What is important for us to remember from this brief survey is that ancient cosmologic speculation, and thus eventually astrology, was the result of philosophic considerations on the nature of the universe and the relationship of man to powers beyond the range of his consciousness. In short, the parents of astrology were not the magicians and charlatans, but the philosophers.

But before we can test the value of the astrological system and the objections leveled against it, we must first acquaint ourselves with the astrological universe itself.

The Universe of Astrology

The impression that the sun travels westward through the sky, around the earth, is caused by the eastward

---

6 The reader wishing to pursue Ptolemy's rationale will find a simplified exposition in Arthur Koestler, *The Sleepwalkers* (New York: Grosset & Dunlap, 1963).

movement of the earth as it rotates on its axis. This apparent movement of the sun through the heavens gave rise to the idea of its having a path or course within which it perpetually travels that astronomers call the *ecliptic,* the line upon which eclipses might occur. The astrologer locates the ecliptic within a broader band or belt called the zodiac. It is within the confines of this belt that the major planets tend to travel.

The term "zodiac" is of Greek origin and roughly translates as "circle of signs" or "circle of sculptured figures (animals)." This term was first used and, we must assume, created by Aristotle in the fourth century before our era. To the Babylonians, the original creators of this imaginary band girding the earth, it was simply known as Anu's way, Anu being the sky god.

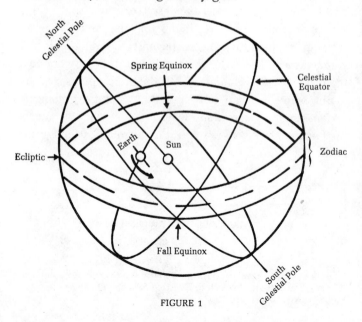

FIGURE 1

The delineation of Anu's way had taken place as early as 700 B.C. The following allusion to it is made in the Babylonian creation epic:

He constructed stations for the great god,
Fixing their astral likenesses as constellations.
He determined the year by designating the zones.
He set up three constellations for each of the twelve months.
After defining the days of the year by means of heavenly figures
He found the station of Nebiru (Jupiter) to determine the heavenly bands,
That none might transgress or fall short.[7]

The "beginning" of this imaginary belt was chosen arbitrarily and is thought to represent the birth of the year, the vernal equinox, when day and night are of equal length all over the earth. This is the season of spring and coincides with March 21. On a horoscope this point is referred to as the ascendant.

Traveling approximately 1 degree each day, the sun is thought to traverse 90 degrees of the zodiac in order to arrive at the *imum coeli,* or nadir, around June 21, the summer solstice. As it travels toward this point the sun is thought to increase in potency until it reaches its fullest form. From here on, it begins to wane in power. Progressing another 90 degrees, it arrives at the point known as the descendant, the fall equinox, which occurs about September 23. Its potency declines even more

---

[7] "Akkadian Myths and Epics," trans. by E. A. Speiser, in James B. Pritchard, ed., *Ancient Near Eastern Texts Relating to the Old Testament* (3rd ed.; Princeton, N.J.: Princeton University Press, 1969), p. 67.

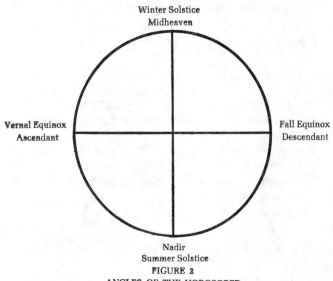

Winter Solstice
Midheaven

Vernal Equinox
Ascendant

Fall Equinox
Descendant

Nadir
Summer Solstice
FIGURE 2
ANGLES OF THE HOROSCOPE

drastically as it approaches the *medium coeli,* or midheaven, about December 21, the winter solstice, where
it experiences its death.

What has just been outlined in discussing the apparent path of the sun during the course of a year are the
four angles of a horoscope. Each of the 90-degree angles, in turn, is broken down into three sectors of 30 degrees each, the length of an astrological month. Each of
the twelve sectors (a house) houses a sign, the astrological notations of which are given in Figure **3**.

The original Babylonian titles of these signs were es-
tablished by 419 B.C. in the following order: Aries,
Pleiades, Gemini, Praesepe, Leo, Spica, Libra, Scorpio,
Sagittarius, Capricornus, Aquarius, and Pisces. The

Aries ♈	Libra ♎
Taurus ♉	Scorpio ♏
Gemini ♊	Sagittarius ♐
Cancer ♋	Capricorn ♑
Leo ♌	Aquarius ♒
Virgo ♍	Pisces ♓

FIGURE 3

Greeks later substituted Taurus, Cancer, and Virgo for Pleiades, Praesepe, and Spica. Otherwise, the basic form of the zodiac as devised by the Babylonians has remained to this day.[8]

As the sun progresses through the sky during the course of a year it "passes through the signs" at a speed of approximately 1 degree a day, or 30 degrees a month. The sign that the sun is "in" at the birth of an individual is what traditionally determines the astrological sign of that person. Therefore, one born on March 25 of any year would be an Aries because according to traditional astrology the sun on that date has as its backdrop the constellation of the Ram, symbolic animal of Aries. But because of the phenomenon known as the precession of the equinoxes, the sun's backdrop on March 25 is actually the constellation Pisces. We will see below why this is the case, but note in the meantime that most astrologers today ignore the circumstances brought about by the precession and claim that the traditional system should remain unchanged. It is, in fact, this very phenomenon that is the basis for claims by modern-day

[8] For the position and relationship between signs, planets, and houses and all other astrological terms, see Appendix A.

skeptics that astrology has no real foundation. It should also be mentioned that the skeptics I refer to are not just those who casually reject astrology out of hand, but also some contemporary astrologers who base the construction of their horoscopes on the reality of the precession. So, we have three warring factions: those who do not believe in astrology at all, those astrologers who have corrected their computations to include the shift in constellations, and the traditionalists who insist that the original and older system is still viable regardless of the facts. Let us now explore the facts behind the creation of the second zodiac brought about by the precession.

The Precession of the Equinoxes

In the year 130 B.C. the Greek astronomer Hipparchus of Nicaea noticed a star where he was certain none had existed before. At the time of this discovery he had already computed the distance between the earth and the moon, making an error of only 5 percent; determined the solar year as being 365¼ days minus 4 minutes and 48 seconds, only 6 minutes short of modern-day calculations; and reckoned the mean lunar month at 29 days, 12 hours, 44 minutes, and 2½ seconds, missing the correct figure by only 1 second. It was not unusual for a man of such determination to then systematically plot and record the celestial latitude and longitude of 1,080 fixed stars in an attempt to discover exactly how he could have missed the star. Comparing his catalog with that of Timochares, drawn up 166 years earlier, he confirmed not only that the star had only recently appeared but also that all of the stars concerned had shifted their positions by 2 degrees. In short, he discovered that the stars were not as "fixed" as tradition had believed them to be. This phenomenon has come to be called the precession of the equinoxes, the equinoxes ("equal nights") signifying places where the sun appears to cross the equator during its northward and southward passages. The northward movement is known as the vernal equinox and occurs on March 21; the southern, the autumnal, taking place on September 22.

To be explicit, the equinoxes represent the two times when the celestial equator and the ecliptic touch (see Figure 1, page 28). If the 23½-degree tilt of the earth's axis did not exist and the celestial equator and the ecliptic were equal, touching one another at all points, we would not experience seasonal changes. It is this tilt that causes the earth to wobble in the manner of a spinning top that is slowing down, thus causing the earth's axis to circumscribe a circle in the heavens. For this reason the star closest to the earth's axis, the polestar, changes every so many thousand years. Five thousand years ago the polestar was Alpha Draconis. The star presently closest to the earth's axial wobble is Alpha Ursa Minoris, also known as Polaris, which will be replaced by the star Vega in A.D. 14,000. Since the revolution of the earth's axis takes about 25,800 years, Polaris will not be the polestar again until A.D. 28,000.

Less than two thousand years ago, somewhere around A.D. 220, the vernal equinox actually occurred against the backdrop of the constellation Aries. Since that time there has been a shift of approximately 25 degrees in the tilt of the earth's axis. This is the significance and effect of the precession of the equinoxes.

We are left with two zodiacs. That based on the actual position of the stars is called the sidereal zodiac, which moves forward one day every seventy-two years. Hipparchus originally calculated this movement at thirty-six seconds a year against our present-day calculation of fifty.

The second zodiac, which is invariably associated with Ptolemy, and which the great majority of astrologers rely on, is called the tropical zodiac. Hipparchus himself suggested the creation of this zodiac, for by it, he rightly believed, a reasonably dependable seasonal calendar could be created. The tropical zodiac does not rely on the position of the stars but instead is based on the passage of the sun over four critical points: the solstices (the tropic of Cancer and the tropic of Capricorn) and the equinoxes. At first sight the discrepancies between these two markedly different zodiacs would appear to substantiate the skeptic's claim that the theories of astrology are untenable. After all, if a so-called Aries is a Pisces according to the sidereal zodiac, how then can traditional astrology support the contention that its methods are based on observation and fact? What has been continually overlooked in this debate is that the precession of the equinoxes has absolutely no effect on the manifestation of the seasons themselves and that it is upon this phenomenon that tropical astrology bases itself.

In short, tropical astrology was and is concerned with the apparent coincidence of certain psychological and biologic types being born at specific *seasons* and not with the positions of the fixed stars:

Early civilizations were closer to nature and consequently imputed greater importance to the sun cycle; . . . It is psychologically understandable—for no better system of reference was available—that the observation even of small effects should have given rise to the inference that the entire earthly and celestial world is governed by the cycles of the solar system and constellations. Thus the solar "cosmic systems" of ancient civilizations and the early astrology that formed a part of them should be regarded neither as mere superstition nor purely as psychological projection or theological symbolism, but must be interpreted in part as a speculative attempt to derive the whole structure of the material and psychic world from comparatively small solar effects on man and nature. Some of these early systems have a far more real and empirical character than the later, largely astrological, cosmologies.[9]

Such observations of the sun's effect on man and his environment are essentially what gave birth to the science of astrology. And here it must be emphasized that at one time it was legitimate to think of astrology as a science, for it did indeed for a short period of time record empirical facts. However, with the shifting of the equinoxes the symbolic parameters once given these observations were no longer deemed viable. This decision was not based on scientifically determined data, but rather on the grounds that astrology could no longer conform to logical formulae.

Logic won out, and there the argument would have

[9] Max Knoll, "Transformations of Science in Our Age," in Joseph Campbell, ed., *Man and Time: Eranos Yearbook 3*, trans. by Ralph Manheim (New York: Pantheon Books, 1957), p. 304.

ended if not for the findings of the empiricists themselves centuries later, findings based solely on sidereal
events shorn of metaphysics or religion.

Because at one time the tropical and sidereal zodiacs
corresponded with one another, and because there is, as
we shall see, evidence that the sidereal zodiac does affect
us, we may assume that the typologies recorded in classical astrological books were at one time viable realities
—that there once was a correspondence between the
human body and the events of the heavens. Currently,
little of the scientific research being conducted dealing
with meteorological effects on the physiological and psychological systems of man attempts to correlate its findings with tropical astrology, although several researchers
do find cause to refer to sidereal astrology. To conclude
that early astrology was simply the classification of
meteorological effects on man does not answer the questions we posed earlier: How are we still to find relevance in an astrology that does not base itself on the
sidereal heavens? Why do astrologers insist that Ptolemaic astrology still works even though it no longer
corresponds with the true events occurring in the heavens? and How are we to reconcile this with the findings
supporting the veracity of a sidereal zodiac, findings
that to all appearances contradict the positions of classical astrologers?

Our first objective will be an inquiry into the evidence substantiating the idea that the operations of the
sidereal universe affect us. Much of this evidence, which
has been squirreled away in scientific journals, will indicate to what degree these influences operate. Then we
shall proceed to analyze the symbolic elements of the

Ptolemaic system in search of the psychic constituents we believe are contained therein.

This position requires some further amplification, and what I would like to propose at this point is that there is and has always been an organizer of unconscious perceptive functions in man that either seeks or contrives to find in *natural* phenomena a correspondence through which it may symbolically display itself. It may be inspired by external stimuli that display a pattern of organization similar to itself. In the beginning we may have been available to stimuli of a lower frequency. The earlier and more psychic receptive mechanisms may no longer be available to the lower frequencies of such stimuli. And here I specifically refer to those mechanisms or operations that reside at the unconscious levels of our psyches. The suggestion here is that of the two human systems, the psychic and the somatic, the former is the earliest and that which, possibly with the advent of "civilization," has receded into the background of our being for subtler operations. That the subtler spiritual substance of being would predate the secondary material substance has also been suggested by Teilhard de Chardin:

> Because matter can be touched, and because it *appears* historically to have existed first, it is accepted without examination as the primordial stuff and most intelligible portion of the cosmos. But *this road leads nowhere.* Not only does matter, the symbol for multiplicity and transience, escape the direct grasp of thought, but, more disadvantageously still, this same matter shows itself incapable by its very nature of giving rise to the world that surrounds us

and gives us substance. It is radically impossible to conceive that interiorized and spontaneous elements could ever have developed from a universe presumed in its initial state to have consisted entirely of determinisms. . . . A universe whose primal stuff is matter is irremediably fixed and sterile; whereas a universe of "spiritual" stuff has all the elasticity it would need to lend itself both to evolution (life) and to involution (entropy).[10]

But to support such a proposal, assuming that such receptive mechanisms do not fade into oblivion out of disuse any more than one's appendix does, we would first have to find scientific evidence to corroborate what at first sight appears to be a metaphysical statement.

The following pages will in large part be dedicated to the findings of empirical science and will be presented with one end in mind: to propose that in the effects of the phenomena caused by the sidereal and the Ptolemaic zodiacs we are faced with two operations of a distinctly unique nature, and that both of them are legitimate if applied to their respective areas of influence.

In the sidereal zodiac value may be found in the suggestion that the operations of the cosmos most affect the faculties of our physiological natures. With reference to the classical or tropical zodiac, we suggest that there is a psychic ground that at base is in no way affected by the sidereal universe, but is instead a totally independent system, with its own end. This conclusion will be based on the idea that the original astrological metaphysic was a mythos in which the operations of the heavens were

[10] Teilhard de Chardin, *Human Energy* (New York: Harcourt Brace Jovanovich, 1969), pp. 22–23.

understood as a display of the gods, who in several ways affected and limited human emotions, sensations, and instincts. It is doubtful that Babylonian astrology much concerned itself with these zodiacal effects upon man to the degree that later astrology did. When such effects did become noticeably prominent to the ancient mind, the sidereal zodiac and the tropical zodiac coincided.

Thus, the Ptolemaic system contains within it, beneath the confustion of its sidereal information describing the effects of the heavens upon our biology, an original archetype whose structure is totally symbolic and psychic in origin. Therefore we must approach the Ptolemaic system as a psychological reality rather than as an empirically demonstrable and operable cosmology. And in pursuit of the somatic effects of the sidereal system more information is now accessible to us from quarters in the physical and social sciences.

The Season of Birth

In our earlier discussion we took the position that because the precession of the equinoxes has no effect on the phenomenon of the seasons, a phenomenon upon which Ptolemaic astrology is based, the argument that tropical astrology cannot work because it is inconsistent with the facts of the sidereal heavens holds no water. Skeptics do continue to argue, however, that season of birth can tell us nothing about either psychological or biological types. Having grasped the ax by the wrong end, they nonetheless continue to wield it. In the past forty years, as we shall see, there have been a number of investigations into this problem, all of which appear to substantiate the Ptolemaic view.

In 1928 Edward Huntington, after studying thousands of birth dates in his attempt to discover if there was any relationship between season of birth and longevity, discovered that

> in New England . . . the people born in March, and attaining at least the age of 2 years, have lived on an average nearly four years longer than similar people born in July. Length of life depends upon the combined effect of many causes; the investigations here described show that season of birth must be added to the causes already known.[11]

In that same work Huntington directs our attention to the work of another researcher who

> tabulated the intelligence quotients of thousands of school children in or near New York. He found that on an average the children born in May and June and also in September and October have a slightly higher IQ than those born at other seasons. Among the 17,000 children whom he investigated, the average intelligence quotient was lowest among those born in January and February.[12]

In both instances season of birth appeared to have a marked influence on both longevity and intelligence. In neither case, however, was there an attempt to discover a cause for such effects.

In a work entitled *The Patient and the Weather*, W.

[11] Edward Huntington, *Season of Birth: Its Relation to Human Abilities* (New York: John Wiley, 1938), p. 86.

[12] *Ibid.*, p. 184.

F. Petersen, pursuing the idea that there may be certain physiological types who are affected by the influence of the sun on the environment, theorized that such individuals could have been permanently "imprinted" by meteorological influences during the prenatal period.[13] This would have been brought about by a stimulation of the developing cells and organs in such a way as to cause them later to respond either positively or negatively to excesses or deficiencies of available active oxygen in the atmosphere. This phenomenon, it was later surmised, is brought about by the emission of solar ion "beam clouds" during sunspot activity.[14] (That the human system is capable not only of being influenced by ionization but also of distinguishing between positive and negative ions has been substantiated by A. Krueger and R. Smith.[15]) Gustave Bergmann referred to this type as the "meteorologically stigmatized," pointing out that this group is chiefly to be found in cities, whereas the "diffuse" opposite types—those not stigmatized—appear most frequently in the country. To this we may add Petersen's statement that the former, imprinted, group consists not only of a broad sampling of psychotics, healthy persons, and people particularly sensitive to climatic change, but unusually gifted personalities as well.

[13] W. F. Petersen, *The Patient and the Weather* (Ann Arbor, Mich.: Edwards Brothers, 1934).

[14] Throughout this discussion of ionization and its effects on human physiology, I am indebted to Max Knoll's "Transformations of Science in Our Age," in *Man and Time*, pp. 264–307.

[15] A. Krueger and R. Smith, "The Physiological Significance of Positive and Negative Ionization of the Atmosphere," in *Man's Dependency on the Earthly Atmosphere* (New York: Macmillan, 1962).

In correlating an immense amount of scientific data, Max Knoll mentions that because diametrically opposed responses to negative and positive ion conditions have been scientifically substantiated, there may actually be two different "ion-conditioned" types of personalities in addition to the diffuse, or nonimprinted, type proposed by Bergmann. One type may be negatively stimulated to yield the mentally disturbed, the other positively stimulated to result in the unusually gifted.[16] If this were so, then we would expect to find a maximum of gifted personalities born during one particular season, and this does appear to be the case. In the table on page 44 the Nobel prizewinners in physics and chemistry are presented according to season of birth.

Knoll himself points out that the sampling is small but adds that Petersen's research dealt with thousands of persons and yielded the same correspondence between season of birth and ability.

There is an increasing belief that not only season of birth but also yearly fluctuation in climate greatly affect both our psychological and physiological conditions. What is important to note in our survey up to this point is the fact that the research data discussed above had ultimately to do with seasonal effects occurring at the time of the equinoxes and solstices, and that a good many researchers concerned themselves with the effects of the sun. As we have pointed out, this is essentially

[16] Dr. Heinz Lehman, of the Douglas Hospital in Montreal, in an unpublished paper the results of which are reported in Gay Gaer Luce, *Body Time: Physiological Rhythms and Social Stress* (New York: Pantheon Books, 1971), reports that in trying to discover the cause of periodic outbursts of hostility among some of his ward patients, he discovered that the outbursts corresponded to the occurrence of sunspots.

what the Ptolemaic system was concerned with—events brought about by the passage of the sun across the equinoxes and the solstices.

Another and far more impressive statistical survey was undertaken by the French statistician Michel Gauquelin some twenty years ago. Gauquelin set out to disprove the claims of astrology, and it was only after exhaustive research that he later concluded that there *was* a relationship between man and the stars. Gauquelin's statistical analysis dealt with the angular configurations, or "aspects," the planets take up in relation to one another and the traditionally expected result. (See Appendix A.)

During a chart analysis of 576 members of the French Academy of Medicine, Gauquelin unwittingly discovered a high incidence of the planets Mars and Saturn "aspecting" the ascendants and descendants of the horoscopes in question. Comparing them with the horoscopes of "normal" and undistinguished personalities chosen at random from census records, he discovered that the latter group of "normals" did not have a higher birth incidence when the two planets were aspecting their ascendants and descendants. Pressing further, he chose and analyzed a new sample of 508 famous physicians—with the same results.

Between 1950 and 1960 Gauquelin, after computing the horoscopes of famous Frenchmen, traveled to Italy, Germany, Belgium, and Holland to compile a list of twenty-five thousand birth dates, this time including politicians, athletes, actors, military men, and writers, among other occupational groups.

A new picture began to emerge. The samplings of physicians still showed the above-chance aspecting of

DISTRIBUTION OF THE BIRTH DATES OF NOBEL PRIZE WINNERS
IN PHYSICS AND CHEMISTRY, 1901–1939 °

Before and after vernal equinox (Feb. 5–May 6)	*Before and after autumnal equinox* (Aug. 7–Nov. 7)	*Before and after the summer solstice* (May 7–Aug. 6)	*Before and after the winter solstice* (Nov. 8–Feb. 4)
Arrhenius	Anderson	Barkla	Becquerel
W. L. Bragg	Aston	W. H. Bragg	Dalén
Butenandt	Baeyer	Braun	Haber
Debye	Bergius	Buchner	Heisenberg
Einstein	Bohr	P. Curie	Langmuir
Von Euler-Chelpin	Bosch	H. Fischer	Michelson
Grignard	L. de Broglie	Hertz	Rayleigh
Guillaume	Chadwick	Hess	Richards
Haworth	A. H. Compton	Lenard	Siegbahn
F. Joliot-Curie	M. Curie	Lorentz	J. J. Thomson
Karrer	Davisson	Nernst	Van der Waals
Marconi	Dirac	Wieland	Werner
Millikan	Fermi	Zeeman	Wien
Planck	E. Fischer		Windaus
Richardson	J. Franck		
Roentgen	Harden		
Stark	I. Joliot-Curie		
G. P. Thomson	Kamerlingh-Onnes		
Urey	Von Laue		
Wallach	Lawrence		
Wilson	Lippmann		
Zsigmondy	Moissan		
	Ostwald		
	Perrin		
	Pregl		
	Raman		
	Ramsay		
	Rutherford		
	Ruzicka		
	Sabatier		
	Schrödinger		
	Soddy		
	Svedberg		
	Van't Hoff		
	Willstätter		
TOTAL 22	TOTAL 35	TOTAL 13	TOTAL 14

GRAND TOTAL 84

Summary: Born before and after the equinoxes: $22 + 35 = 57$ or 68% of 84.
Born before and after the solstices: $13 + 14 = 27$ or 32% of 84.

° From Knoll, "Transformations of Science in Our Age," p. 303.

Saturn and Mars mentioned above, but different configurations appeared for the other professions:

> a great many individuals born when Mars was ap-
> pearing over the horizon or passing at the highest
> point of its course later became famous doctors,
> great athletes, or military leaders, while future ar-
> tists, painters, or musicians were seldom born at
> the times propitious for doctors and athletes. Actors
> and politicians were born more frequently when Ju-
> piter rose or culminated—but scientists were rarely
> born at that time. Thus, as far as vocational success
> was concerned, the moon, Mars, Jupiter, and Sat-
> urn were found to act as planetary clocks.[17]

These findings were largely ignored by the scientific
community. It was not that scientists doubted Gauquelin's meticulous methodology; they were simply unable
to accept the possibility that astrology might work after
all. Gauquelin, however, continued to provide his colleagues with even more improbabilities: He computed
the charts of fifteen thousand couples and their children
in an attempt to discover if there were any significant
correlations resembling those that astrologers usually
claim. Dealing with over three hundred thousand planetary positions with odds of 500,000 to 1 against the
probability of any above-chance correlations, he found
statistically significant relationships.

Gauquelin, however, does not himself believe in astrology. He subscribes instead to the idea of some as yet
undiscovered scientific laws, insisting that what we are
witness to here are some mysterious phenomena of
hereditable responses to planetary influences. Whereas an

[17] Michel Gauquelin, *The Cosmic Clocks* (Chicago: Henry Reg-
nery, 1967), p. 191.

astrologer would say that the statistically significant correlations between a child's horoscope and his parents'
result from planetary influences present at the time of
birth, Gauquelin has it that "the birth of a child when
Mars appears over the horizon is not mere chance. The
birth occurs at that moment rather than another because
his organism is ready to react to the perturbations
caused by this particular planet at its passage over the
horizon." [18] All of which is somewhat analogous to saying that a leaf doesn't fall to the ground but is instead
pulled toward it by gravity.

All of the research mentioned up to this point appears
to suggest that there are in humans receptors so delicate
that they can be influenced by ionization and the general influence of the sun and aspecting planets. None of
the researchers mentioned set out to prove the existence
of such receptors, since their work was primarily statistical in nature. Moreoever, indications that such receptors
do exist have been found in other areas.

Hidden Receptors

Soviet and American scientists have postulated that
Earth's magnetic field changes make it possible for
animals to measure time and that they have a pronounced effect upon the human brain. Experiments
with pulse stimulation have changed brain-wave
configurations and also subjective time perception.
Acute episodes in mental illness, moreover, have
been correlated with times of magnetic disturbance
by reputable psychiatric researchers. [19]

[18] *Ibid.*, p. 197.
[19] Gay Gaer Luce, *Biological Rhythms in Psychiatry and Medicine* (Chevy Chase, Md.: National Institute of Mental Health,
U.S. Department of Health, Education, and Welfare, 1970), p.
143.

In 1962 Yves Rocard, professor of physics at the Sorbonne, reported evidence for the existence of sensory receptors in man so sensitive as to be able to detect and measure fluctuations of subtle variations in magnetic fields. Willing to test the ancient claim that dowsers, or water witches, were capable of detecting the presence of water beneath the earth, Rocard used a magnetometer to discover that there are changes in terrestrial magnetism wherever there is water. From this he surmised that the nerves and muscles in the arms of dowsers were responding to these changes in the magnetic field. He set out to test his supposition. Employing test subjects who were not professional dowsers and turning them loose on a field where he had earlier planted electric coils that could be independently turned on or off, he discovered that the average subject could detect changes in the magnetic field ranging from about 0.3 to 0.5 milligauss. In other words they were able to detect phenomena generally considered beyond the range of our present sensory abilities.

Another researcher using professional dowsers, Dr. Solco Tromp of Holland, discovered that variations as small as 0.001 gauss could be detected.[20]

Frank A. Brown, Jr., Morrison Professor of Biology at Northwestern University, dedicated to extensive research on the probability of the existence of geophysically dependent clock systems, has stated:

There are good reasons to believe that the living organism relies heavily upon a geophysically-depend-

[20] Solco Tromp, "Review of the Possible Physiological Causes of Dowsing," *International Journal of Parapsychology*, Vol. X, No. 4 (1968), p. 269.

ent clock-system. Indeed, since the organism is such
a delicately poised physicochemical entity as to re-
flect small fluctuations in both identified, and
probably still unidentified, subtle geophysical factors, the question arises as to how essential to life
itself are the various components of the natural geophysical complex of the earth's atmosphere.[21]

Professor Brown also offers the diagram in Figure 4 as
illustrative of his general thesis that

organisms are duplex systems with respect to their
rhythmicity. One may think of any plant or animal

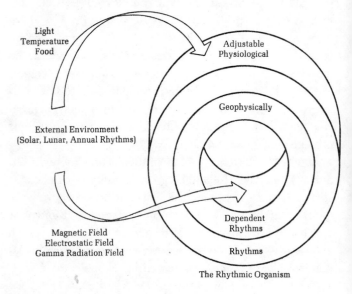

FIGURE 4

[21] Frank A. Brown, Jr., "Response to Pervasive Geophysical Factors and the Biological Clock Problem," *Cold Spring Harbor Symposium on Quantitative Biology,* Vol. XXV (1960), p. 69.

as possessing one rhythmic system underlying another one. . . . The outer ring represents the overt physiological rhythms that we may observe in the organisms in nature and in the laboratory. These are adjustable recurring patterns that can be altered by such factors as changed times of day of 24 hours light-dark cycles, differing photoperiods, temperature changes, times of feeding, and training, thus allowing the organism to adapt to its specifically detailed habitat conditions. Underlying such adjustable physiological rhythms are deep-seated geophysically dependent ones represented by the inner ring. . . . These geophysically dependent rhythms cannot be altered; they are locked into the fluctuations in the earth's geophysical fields to which they are direct, fundamental biological responses.[22]

We can append to this diagram yet another system—the unconscious, or human psyche, or to be more specific, the unconscious system that predates the appearance of consciousness. This system might be placed immediately within and beneath the "geophysically dependent rhythms" and under certain conditions might affect and be affected by the two systems containing it. It would be here that we would find the subtler psychic receptive mechanisms that operate below the threshold of consciousness.

The material discussed up to this point directs us to the existence of subtle receptors of geophysical forces. Other telling evidence substantiates the idea that we are

[22] Frank A. Brown, Jr., "Hypothesis of Environmental Timing of the Clock," in Frank A. Brown, Jr., J. Woodland Hastings, and John D. Palmer, *The Biological Clock: Two Views* (New York: Academic Press, 1970), pp. 26–27.

affected by cosmic influences centered around a major constituent of our bodies—water.

Professor Giorgio Piccardi, director of the Institute of Physical Chemistry at the University of Florence, reports that chemical reactions in water are dependent on the relative positions of the earth, sun, and moon. His fifteen years of research culminated in evidence that chemical reactions are greater when the sun erupts in flares than when it does not. He discovered that there is a correspondence between the rate of acceleration of the speed at which the chemical reactions take place and the occurrence of sunspots in the eleventh and final year of the sunspot cycle.

> We are certain that in the space which surrounds us phenomena occur which influence living beings from afar (and not by contact with material things) by means of radiations or variations in the general field. . . . Electromagnetic radiations and field variations . . . strike the entire mass of a body, and thus of an organism, and provoke the oscillation, excitation or at any rate, the resonance, so to speak, of all the structural elements capable of responding to their stimulus, wherever they are found. . . . Definitely, all living matter reacts to far-off spacial actions, both electromagnetic and field.[23]

If solar eruptions have such a pronounced effect on the water in our bodies after birth, what effect could they conceivably have on the watery beginnings of children in the prenatal stage? Here we refer not just to any one particular organ or set of receptors alone but to the entire structure of our bodies:

[23] Giorgio Piccardi, *The Chemical Basis of Medical Climatology* (Springfield, Ill.: Charles C Thomas, 1962), pp. 124–127.

The action of extraterrestrial forces does not concern any given organ, any given illness, any given biological function, but the complex state of living matter. Organisms have to maintain their vital conditions as far as possible, and to do this they have to react to the fluctuating properties of their environment, to fight in order to keep them stable. This results in a deep-set "fatigue" of all the colloidal system of the organism, of all its material substance. It could be said that it is the living matter as a whole that is so disturbed.[24]

The "Takata reaction," named after Maki Takata, physician and professor at Toho University in Tokyo, is a chemical test employed throughout the world for the testing of albumin in blood serum. The level of this organic colloid was believed to remain constant in men, varying in women according to the menstrual cycle. In short, the amount of albumin in blood serum from year to year, allowing for the fluctuations in women, was a fixed phenomenon throughout the world. However, in January, 1938, all of the hospitals employing the Takata reaction reported that the level of albumin in *both* men and women had suddenly begun to rise without apparent cause. To make matters even more curious, the phenomenon appeared to be worldwide. To substantiate the existence of the phenomenon in his own mind, Takata undertook a four-month experiment with his associate T. Murasugi.

The two men worked a hundred miles apart, each measuring daily the amount of albumin in the male subjects they had employed. At the end of the test period

[24] Giorgio Piccardi, quoted in Gauquelin, *The Cosmic Clocks*, p. 223.

they were both satisfied that the daily variation levels in their subjects' serum did indeed parallel one another.

Takata extended his research and maintained measurements for the next twenty years, noting that the phenomenon occurred only between the periods 1938–1943, and with lesser incidence, 1948–1950. What he considered to be the cause of the fluctuation in albumin levels was the activity of sunspots during two major solar cycles. The number of recorded sunspots for the year 1937 was 114; that for 1947, 150 daily.

That there are sensory receptors lying beyond the range of consciousness capable of detecting and being triggered by subtler influences than we would normally think of appears to gain some credence from such research. We have theorized that these receptive mechanisms may have been unconsciously projected onto external phenomena superficially similar in either cycle or pattern to themselves. They may then have caused certain patterns to become imprinted in the genetic system of man. If such an imprinting did occur, there should be some vestige of these imprints in humans today. We shall now turn our survey to the possible discovery of such imprints.

The Navigation of Birds and the Control of Menstruation

The fact that birds navigate by the sun was well established by the physiologist Gustav Kramer,[25] but this research did not shed any light on how nocturnal migrators orient themselves. It came as a great surprise to the

[25] See Ritchie R. Ward, *The Living Clocks* (New York: Alfred A. Knopf, 1971), pp. 165–185.

scientific community when several years later E. G. Franz Sauer and his wife, Eleanore, published findings that flatly proved birds navigate at night by the stars.

The Sauers had at their disposal the Obers Planetarium in Bremen, Germany, in which they placed warblers under a sky adjusted to the seasonal patterns that would normally be found in nature. The flight direction assumed by the birds duplicated that taken in nature. When a blackcap was placed under a simulated spring sky, the bird set its flight direction to the northeast as it would under normal conditions. Sudden changes in the sky pattern were immediately countered by corrected flight directions. One's immediate reaction to this might be to say that the birds had been imprinted by their *social* environment. But the Sauers conducted one more final and telling experiment with a whitethroat that had been raised from the egg. Though it had never been out of a cage, much less under the open sky, the bird was put through its paces in the planetarium. After the researchers had tested the bird under several simulated sky conditions, they were forced to accept the fact that in every instance the bird made flight-direction adjustments. These adjustments resulted in a course that would have brought the bird to the headwaters of the Nile—the desired destination for the migratory pattern of the season depicted by the planetarium stars. This was no learned response. Genetic imprinting of the pattern of the sky is certainly a strong possibility. Is it also possible that the Ptolemaic zodiac may have been in like manner imprinted in man? Even if this were a possibility, wouldn't such an imprint have fallen into disuse and disappeared in time? Robert Ardrey in his *African Gen-*

esis relates an interesting event that sheds some light on the possible answer to this question.

While visiting a colleague in the field, Ardrey was shown what at first sight appeared to be a very intricately designed and patterned flower. Suddenly his friend waved his hand, and all that remained of the flower was a twig. The flower had been a device of a group of beetles that quickly reformed to create it again. The flower, the anthropologist was told, no longer existed—it was extinct—but the beetles kept repeating the pattern nonetheless. So too may the subtle psychic receptors in man correspond to an outmoded "pattern," the tropical zodiac. But our examples up to this point have been of birds and beetles. Is there any evidence that such a thing could happen in man? This question brings us to research recently done on the control of ovulation by light.

The average woman has a menstrual cycle of 29.5 days, some women varying from 16 to 75 days. The physicist Edmond Deway, working on the principle that light affects the neuroendocrine system, most probably by direct stimulation of the pineal gland as we shall discuss below, began experiments in 1965 with a woman whose history of menstrual irregularity ranged over a period of sixteen years. Her menstrual cycle fluctuated between 23 and 48 days. He discovered that by subjecting the sleeping woman's face to the reflected light of a hundred-watt bulb during the fourteenth, fifteenth, and sixteenth nights of her cycle, her cycle became regulated to 29 days. This same method was employed with similar results on seventeen women patients by Dr. John Rock at the Rock Reproductive Clinic in Boston. Of the seventeen women placed under the light regimen, only two did not achieve the 29-day cycle.

It is apparent that the adjusted menstrual cycles achieved correspond to the moon's cycle of 29.5 days. What we are witness to here is the phenomenon of an earlier entrainment to the lunar period sometime in our prehistory. Obviously, at least in modern-day civilization, the rhythm is no longer phase-locked, a condition that may be attributed to the fact that man now controls his environment at a constant level.

It is a matter of observation that most creatures, humans included, are subject to photoperiodism, the response to seasonal changes in the course of a day via the increase and decrease of light. That such reactions are not limited to organisms with retinal photoreceptors is also apparent when one considers the response of the vegetable kingdom to light. It has also been known for some time that among amphibians, fishes, and reptiles nonretinal responses to photoperiodicity occur as a result of the stimulation by direct light of the pineal organ located in the top of the brain.

Earlier researchers assumed that the pineal body was activated by the passage of light messages through the optic tract, and the messages were then distributed in the ganglia located in the upper portion of the neck and in the superior cervical ganglia. It was believed that in the transmission of these light messages the sympathetic nervous system was activated and in turn somehow informed the pineal gland. But there was one puzzling problem: Creatures whose optical systems had become accidentally or experimentally dysfunctional continued to respond to light. As early as 1935 Jacques Benoit discovered the light-sensitive area in the brain of a Peking duck that responded to direct light. This was the first indication that retinal photoreceptors in animals were not totally responsible for responses to light.

Working with experimentally blinded birds, Michael Menaker discovered that light enters the brains of birds *directly through the skull*.[26] Exposure of the pineal body, as in the Benoit experiments, was not necessary. The experimental methods employed to substantiate this claim are lengthy, so the reader must be referred to the article itself.

Menaker went one step further—he and his co-worker Henry Keatts removed the pineal gland and discovered that photoperiodicity still occurred. His conclusions were as follows:

> The experiments described here, in addition to rais-
> ing many specific questions concerning the ways in
> which environmental light cycles control rhythmic
> and reproductive events, underline the fact, of more
> general concern to biologists, that energy in the vis-
> ible portion of the spectrum may well have effects
> on the activities of the cells once thought to be com-
> pletely shielded from it.[27]

All of this appears to suggest that physiological and chemical responses in an organism that are activated by light received in nonretinal photoreceptors (as yet uni-identified by science) are part of the "subtle" underlying system we hypothesized earlier. What the exposure to light did in the experiments with women whose men-

[26] Michael Menaker, "Nonvisual Light Reception," *Scientific American,* Vol. CCXXVI (March, 1972), pp. 22–29.

[27] *Ibid.*

strual cycles were irregular was to activate this underlying imprint of a lunar cycle that obviously had at one time structured the menstrual cycle itself, most probably at a time in history when our ancestors were constantly exposed to the open air. As the Sauers' experiments with birds suggest, such patterns of response are genetically transmitted. Humans still contain these patterns and rhythms within them, beyond the range of their secondary sensory receptors.

The Dream of Ptolemy

The greater portion of our discussion has been spent attempting to substantiate the proposal that the sidereal zodiac has some basis in fact. But what of the tropical zodiac? If anything, the material presented up to this point would appear to add even more weight to the arguments of the siderealists and skeptics. Yet it is the method of tropical astrology that has held and fascinated humanity—specifically the symbolic parameters that are absent from the sidereal type. And it is here, in the symbolism of astrology, where we obtain clues as to its meaning.

We opened this chapter with an outline of the philosophic background that culminated in the emergence of astrology as a way of perceiving the relationship between man and the cosmos. The Greeks took the mathematical and observational skills the Babylonians had employed for the creation of astrology and turned them into astronomy. And how was this achieved? Through the magic of speculative imagination. Of course the Greeks performed further and exacting observations, but ultimately the data they acquired was subjected to spec-

ulation of the most curious kind. By the time the peak
was reached in naked-eye observation, the Greeks with
the aid of Socrates had turned their attention inward,
toward the soul. It was inevitable that the theories in
this new area would become associated with cosmologic
speculation. It was at this point that the fine line between astronomy and ancient astrology blurred—the
moment when the theory of the cosmos became associated with the theory of being.

According to all reason astrology should have died
once the facts were known. That it did not implies that
its original philosophic structure contains some truths
that it refuses to let consciousness evade. With all of our
science, our rational approaches to the world, astrology
remains. The entire situation is like a recurring nightmare that most doctors agree serves to force an individual to come to terms with an intense emotional
situation. That there is knowledge below the level of
consciousness is signaled by the dream through which it
makes itself known symbolically.

> But now let us consider what the word "symbol"
> implies. A symbol is an image or an imaginary
> event, standing for a real object or event whereto it
> has some distant resemblance. Now the invention of
> a symbol can only be an act of *thought*—the work
> of some intelligence. Symbols cannot invent them-
> selves; they must be thought out. And the question
> arises: who performs the intelligent act; who thinks
> out the symbol? The answer given by the Freudian
> school is: the subconscious.[28]

[28] Frederik Van Eeden, "A Study of Dreams," in Charles T. Tart,
ed., *Altered States of Consciousness: A Book of Readings* (New
York: John Wiley, 1969), p. 149.

Whatever it is that "thinks out" a symbol has also thought out the entire structure of astrology, the symbols that to a certain degree reveal the lineaments of the dream we call astrology. The dream breaks down into four symbolic parts: a quaternity, a trinity, a duality composed of contraries, and a unity. The most important of these in astrology are the quaternity (the elements) and the unity (the Androgyne). Because all four parts ultimately have their origin and logic in the theory of the elements, we shall concentrate more on the development of that theory, saving our comments on the general nature of the trinity and the contraries for later chapters.

Up until the appearance in 1661 of a work by Robert Boyle entitled *The Sceptical Chymist*, the whole of Western culture was under the Aristotelian illusion that matter was composed of the four elements fire, air, earth, and water. This idea was of central importance to astrology because it was believed that man himself was composed of a combination of these elements in varying degrees.

In the Greek world the entire issue of elemental theory began with Thales' idea that the primary constituent of the world was water. To this Aristotle added: "Certain thinkers say that soul is intermingled in the whole universe, and it is perhaps for that reason that Thales came to the opinion that all things are full of Gods." [29]

Anaximander of Miletus, who offered us a cylindrical view of the universe, made an even further distinction:

[29] Aristotle, *De Anima*, in Richard McKeon, ed., *Introduction to Aristotle* (New York: Modern Library, 1947), p. 169.

The primary matter of the world is not an element we are familiar with, but rather an absolute substance from which the elements themselves are eventually born. He called it the indefinite or the boundless and thought it was not only the animating principle of the universe but also divine. Anaximenes theorized a one-element source and asserted that air was the primary substance of the universe. While in Anaximander the elements were "separated out" from the original absolute substance, in Anaximenes' universe it was *an* element soul, that gave birth to the remaining elements.

To follow was a theory proposing fire as the primary substance of the universe, authored by Heraclitus (c. 535–c. 475 B.C.). No mere animating element, it was a fire characterized by intelligence that acts as a vehicle for the divine soul, which is itself thought of as a metaphysical fire. Standing before this primal substance is an even greater principle—the Logos—which is ever constant behind the eternal exchange of the elements:

> There is exchange of all things for fire and of fire for all things.
> Fire lives in the death of earth, air in the death of fire, water in the death of air, and earth in the death of water.
> Listening not to me but to the Logos, it is wise to acknowledge that all things are one.[30]

Finally, Empedocles (c. 495–c. 435 B.C.) set the stage for the next several centuries by stating that the elements do not change one into the other, but are instead

---

[30] *Heraclitus,* trans. and ed. by Philip Wheelwright (Princeton, N.J.: Princeton University Press, 1959), fragments 28, 34, and 118.

four unchangeable kinds of matter, which, through combination, make up the objects of the world:

> [Empedocles] makes the material elements four in number, fire, air, water and earth, all eternal, but changing its bulk and scarcity through mixture and separation; but his real first principles, which impart motion to these, are Love and Strife. The elements are continually subject to an alternate change, at one time mixed together by Love, at another separated by Strife.[31]

Originally the four elements were contained in total union in a sphere, which was the body of God bound together by love, the soul. Strife poured in on all sides of this reign of love, causing love itself to rush out and meet it. At this point the elements became divided, only to recombine in the shape of mortal forms. It is through these forms that the soul must travel in an almost endless series of transmigrations before it may become reunited with love.

The four-element theory proposed by Empedocles took immediate hold of the Greek imagination, changing little until the appearance of Aristotle (384–322 B.C.). The exception to this was Plato's statement in *The Timaeus* to the effect that God created the universe out of the four elements and

> in the center he put the soul, which he diffused throughout the body, making it also to be the exterior environment of it; and he made the universe a circle moving in a circle, one and solitary, yet by reason of its excellence able to converse with itself,

---

[31] G. S. Kirk and J. E. Raven, *The Pre-Socratic Philosophers* (New York: Cambridge University Press, 1966), pp. 329–330.

and needing no other friendship or acquaintance, having these purposes in view he created the world a blessed god.[32]

Turning to the creation of humans, we are then told that God:

Once more into the cup in which he had previously mingled the soul of the universe . . . poured the remains of the elements, and mingled them in much the same manner; they were not, however, pure as before, but diluted to the second and third degree. And having made it he divided the whole mixture into souls equal in number to the stars and assigned each soul to a star. . . . Now when they should be implanted in bodies . . . it would be necessary that they should all have in them one and the same faculty of sensation, arising out of irresistible impressions; in the second place, they must have love, in which pleasure and pain mingle; also fear and anger, and the feelings akin or opposite to them.[33]

We are later told that this world soul (*anima mundi*) contains within it the whole of the "corporeal universe" and is "interfused everywhere from the center to the circumference of heaven of which also she is the external envelopment, herself turning in herself." [34] So God first created the "body," or *anthropos,* of the universe, in which are contained the stars, the constellations, and the planets. Then He created the force to operate this divine machinery, the soul. One must assume that the

[32] Plato, *The Timaeus*, trans. by Benjamin Jowett (New York: The Liberal Arts Press, 1949), pp. 16–17.
[33] *Ibid.*, p. 24.
[34] *Ibid.*, pp. 18–19.

perfection assigned the *anthropos* can be equaled only by the perfection of the *anima mundi*. When we refer to man the microcosm, we discover that not only were the elements out of which he was created "diluted to the second or third degree," but the allotment of original soul stuff to be mixed with the elements was only the residue contained "in the cup in which he had previously mingled the soul of the universe." In contrast to the macrocosm, the microcosm is weak and imperfect and to that degree is affected by the movements of the heavens. Ptolemy would later enumerate the types of souls that come into being when the planets aspect one another.[35] But the essence of his long explanation will essentially have to do with the *type* of personality that comes into being: the psychological makeup peculiar to each of us.

Aristotle contributed also to an elemental theory, adding the ether, which he believed to be the original matter of the four elements. The elements not only played a formal part in the composition of matter, but also figured in the cosmologic scheme of things in that they were each assigned a sphere of activity in the heavens. The element earth resided at the center of the universe and was surrounded by a circle of water, around which was a layer of air, followed by the element fire. The ether was the fifth and all-containing element, perfect and divine.

But Aristotle's most important contribution to elemental theory by far was the idea that the four elements were distinguished by four qualities: the dry, the hot,

[35] Ptolemy, *Tetrabiblos,* iii, 13–14.

the cold, the fluid or moist. Each element was composed of two of these qualities:

fire = hot and dry   air = hot and fluid
water = cold and fluid   earth = cold and dry

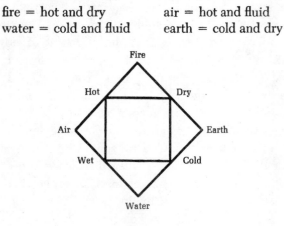

FIGURE 5

These classifications seem to have originated during Empedocles' lifetime in the theories of the physician Hippocrates of Cos (c. 460–c. 370 B.C.). The Hippocratic school believed that the body contained four humors of fluids: blood, phlegm, choler (yellow bile), and black choler (black bile). The identification of the four humors with the four qualities was championed by the Roman physician Galen (A.D. c. 130–c. 200) and became the medical mainstay of the Middle Ages.

The extent to which the correspondence between the elements and man was taken may be seen in an excerpt from the fifteenth-century occultist Henry Cornelius Agrippa:

the eyes, placed in the uppermost place, are the more pure, and have an affinity with the nature of

Fire and Light; then the ears have the second order of purity, and are compared to the Air; the nostrils have the third order, and have a middle nature betwixt the Air and the Water. Last of all the touching is diffused through the whole body, and is compared to the grossness of Earth.[36]

The application of elemental theory to astrology appears to have been Ptolemy's invention. In his system the elements are further differentiated by association with the astrological signs into the categories known as quadruplicities and triplicities (see Appendix A). In comparison with the other occult sciences to be discussed, the metaphysic of trinitarian qualities in astrology is wanted insofar as there is little literature explaining the psychology behind the distribution of the elements and their effects over the zodiac. That there are psychological implications to be had in the system is apparent when one considers that historically this distribution gave rise to carefully outlined personality types.

Included in Ptolemy's *Tetrabiblos* is a detailed explanation of the opposites, the masculine and feminine qualities of the signs. The introduction of the idea of the opposites to theories of cosmology must be credited to Anaximander, who held that the universe came into being via the separating off of the qualities hot and cold from the original substance of the universe. These qualities almost immediately became identified with the sexes —masculine representing the hot and dry; feminine, the cold and moist. In astrology half the astrological signs are identified with the masculine, the other half

[36] Henry Cornelius Agrippa, *Three Books of Occult Philosophy or Magic* (New York: Samuel Weiser, 1971), pp. 190–191.

with the feminine. Which brings us to our next symbol:
the figure of the Androgyne and its place in astrology.

The first mention of the Androgyne in Greek philosophy appears in Plato's *Symposium:*

> The sexes were not two as they are now, but
> originally three in number; there was man, woman,
> and the union of the two, having a name corresponding to this double nature, which had once a
> real existence, but is now lost, and the word "Androgynous" is only preserved as a term of reproach. In
> the second place the primeval man was round, his
> back and sides forming a circle; and he had four
> hands and four feet, one head with two faces looking opposite ways, set on a round neck and precisely alike. . . . Now, the sexes were three . . . because
> the sun, moon, and earth are three; and the man
> was originally the child of the sun, the woman of
> the earth, and the man-woman of the moon, which
> is made up of sun and earth, and they were all
> round.[37]

In time the Demiurge splits these figures in half to
create men and women, each from then on seeking their
counterparts.

The astrological archetype as it exists today can be
seen as a symbol of the original wholeness that Plato referred to. In it we find not only the opposites, the four
elements he spoke of as composing man, but an animating principle in the form of the soul. The following,
from the Roman astrologer Manilius, written about a
century and a half before the birth of Ptolemy, is believed to be the first description of the Androgyne as an
astrological figure, the heavenly man of the Middle Ages:

[37] *The Works of Plato,* ed. by Irwin Edman (New York: Modern
Library, 1928), pp. 353–354.

Now learn what signs the several Limbs obey,
Whose Powers they feel, and where Obedience pay.
The *Ram* defends the *Head*, the *Neck* the *Bull*,
The *Arms*, bright *Twins*, are subject to your Rule:
In the *Shoulders Leo*, and the *Crab's* obeyed
In the *Breast*, and in the *Guts* the modest *Maid*:
In the *Buttocks Libra*, *Scorpio* warms Desires
In *Secret Parts*, and spreads unruly Fire:
The *Thighs* the *Centaur*, and the *Goat* commands
The *Knees*, and binds them up in double Bands.
The parted *Legs* in moist *Aquarius* meet,
And *Pisces* gives Protection to the *Feet*.[38]

There is a very orderly creation myth in all of this
material. At the beginning of the universe there stands a
hermaphroditic figure containing within itself in perfect
harmony all that is to be. Its first operation is the division of itself into the opposites: male-female, hot-cold,
dark-light, etc. This mode then gives way to a trinitarian
operation that takes several forms: three parts of the
soul, three divisions of the world (animal, vegetable,
mineral), and the three-fold distribution of the elements
(whose appearance is the final operation). All of these
operations are found in the archetype of astrology, which
refers us to an active state of order:

In the first place you must know that God, that arti-
ficer of man, has produced under the direction of
Nature the form of man and his whole stature and
substance after the pattern and fashion of the
world. He has compounded man's frame, as that of
the world, out of the four elements, fire and water,
air and earth, so that out of the mixture of these he

[38] *The Five Books of M. Manilius*, trans. by "T.C." (Washington:
National Astrological Library, 1953), p. 72.

might equip a living being after the divine fashion. He compounded man by divine handiwork, so that within the small compass of his body he might bestow under the requirements of Nature the whole energy and substance of the elements, thus preparing an abode, frail if you please but similar to that of the world, for that divine spirit which came down from the celestial mind to sustain the mortal body. So man, as a microcosm, is sustained by the five planets and the sun and moon by their fiery and eternal motion, so that as a being endowed with life after the fashion of the world he should be controlled by the same divine substance.[39]

The diagrammatic figure we are left with is a cosmic diagram that purports to contain within it a schema of all operations that may transpire at either the cosmic or mundane level. As such, the archetypal figure when employed as a horoscope may be seen as an instrument of knowledge used to reveal aspects of one's personality thought to be concealed from consciousness. The information thus acquired can only be thought of as having been given by a transpersonal source whose operations manifest themselves in the heavens first before manifesting themselves on earth. Furthermore, one acquires a certain degree of invulnerability by aligning oneself with the operations of this cosmic diagram by assuming familiarity with the perambulations of the heavens through an "understanding" of the relativity of the suprapersonal to the personal. It is in regard to these two levels of meaning that the astrological archetype an-

[39] Firmicus Maternus, quoted in Jack Lindsay, *The Origins of Astrology* (London: Frederick Muller, 1971), p. 122.

swers the description of similar figures known in the East as mandalas.

The Mandala of the Ordering Principle

Simply defined, the term "mandala" is a Tibetan term meaning "magic circle" and refers to ritual diagrams or objects employed in meditation for the purpose of reuniting the devotee with the cosmos. Mandalas are generally either circular or square but may take a variety of forms as long as they contain those features which properly identify them as mandalas. In order for such devices to qualify as such, they must symbolize the central axis of the cosmos, depict the union of opposites, equate cosmic space and time with temporal space and time (the compass points, the seasons, ages), be symbolic of a divine being whose physical features correspond to the human body, be illustrative of energies or powers at both the cosmic and mundane levels (this includes variations on the senses, instincts, moods, and psychological temperaments), and have their structural components based on multiples of either three or four. There are other features that often appear in mandalic construction, such as color, number, letters of the alphabet, musical tones, divinities, etc., but those mentioned above are the major distinguishing features appearing in mandalas all over the world.

Comparing this list of identifying features with the astrological archetype, one will discover that it corresponds to the description of a mandala in every instance. But, one may rightly ask, what is the point of this correspondence if mandalas appear to be little more than intellectual constructions, philosophically constructed mnemonic devices? If mandalas were nothing more than consciously constructed devices, there would be no significance. But this is not the case.

The Indologist Heinrich Zimmer's account of a Buddhist's experience of the mandala is that he "develops out of and around himself an image of the world with the Mountain of the Gods, Sumeru, in the midst." [40] In a detailed exposition of the ritual an initiate must perform prior to the construction of a mandala, Professor Giuseppe Tucci concludes:

> From the spirit of the mystic who is absorbed in the contemplation which transports him on to the plane of eternal existence, there blazes forth, shining round about, the divine matrices of things. He sees them issue from him and re-enter him in that symbol which religious experience has fixed in definite forms. . . . The images that the mystic sees come forth from the centre of his own heart pervade space and then re-absorb themselves in him. . . . Therefore, the process reveals itself to the eyes of the mystic who has been duly initiated as an immense mobile mandala.[41]

Because the mandalas produced during such rites more often than not coincide in form and content with existing traditional designs, one may argue that such initiations do nothing more than give the initiate the illusion that the mandala is being produced. Though there may be some truth to this, it does not explain the ap-

---

[40] Paraphrased in C. G. Jung and C. Kerenyi, *Essays on a Science of Mythology* (New York: Harper Torchbooks, 1963), p. 13.
[41] Giuseppe Tucci, *The Theory and Practice of the Mandala* (New York: Samuel Weiser, 1970), pp. 105–106.

pearance of such structures in the dreams and visions of Westerners ignorant of Eastern doctrine and practice.

C. G. Jung discovered such forms emerging from the psyches of his European patients, the majority of whom knew nothing about mandalas. He observed that during certain states of the analytic procedure, those particularly marked by issues of extreme crisis or conflict, the majority of his patients dreamed of extraordinarily detailed images that defied interpretation by conventional analytic methods. The production of these mandalas came to his attention "long before I knew their meaning or their connection with the strange practices of the East, which, at that time, were wholly unfamiliar to me." [42] After many years of consideration he concluded that in any deep penetration of the unconscious the individual suffers a disorientation of his conscious personality, a decentering. The appearance of the mandala at such times is the psyche's announcement that an attempt is being made at the unconscious level to rearrange and reintegrate those components of the ego that "break down" or "fly to pieces." The visual representation of this psychological process is the mandala.

One may distinguish three types of mandalas: (1) those which are to some extent prompted by and artistically controlled through religious ritual and doctrine; (2) those which spontaneously appear in the psyches of individuals; and (3) those which spontaneously appear at the collective level.

The astrological archetype of Ptolemaic astrology is a mandala of the third type, its appearance being

---

[42] Richard Wilhelm and C. G. Jung, *The Secret of the Golden Flower* (New York: Wehman Bros., 1955), p. 99.

prompted by the same conditions that cause mandalas to appear in the psyches of individuals: a crisis or conflict, but at the collective level. We shall reserve mention of the collective crisis that caused this mandala to appear in history for our next chapter.

We have already suggested several times the existence of an organizer of unconscious perceptive functions, an ordering principle whose lineaments are symbolically displayed in the archetype of Ptolemaic astrology. Anaxagoras had an intimation of this idea when he stated: "At first all things were together in an indiscriminate mixture. Then came Nous and arranged them in order." [43] This is a particularly enlightening statement, for it corresponds to Jung's contention that mandalas—symbols of order—arise during moments of crisis, internal chaos, or what Anaxagoras terms "indiscriminate mixture." What brings order to the chaotic moment is nous, mind, of a higher order than that normally allotted the consciousness of humans.

Jung, approaching the issue of God from a purely scientific point of view, postulated the existence of a superordinate principle of order residing at the base of the psyche that he called the self: "The self is not only the centre but also the whole circumference which embraces both conscious and unconscious; it is the centre of this totality, just as the ego is the centre of the conscious mind." [44]

[43] Quoted in Robert Adamson, *The Development of Greek Philosophy* (London: William Blackwood & Sons, 1908), p. 49.

[44] C. G. Jung, *The Collected Works of C. G. Jung*, ed. by G. Adler, M. Fordham, H. Read, and W. McGuire, trans. by R. F. C. Hull, Vol. XII: *Psychology and Alchemy* (London: Routledge & Kegan Paul, 1953), p. 41.

"It embraces not only the conscious but also the unconscious psyche, and is therefore, so to speak, a personality which we *also* are." [45] Thus, an early Greek text tells us, as so many Oriental texts do, "If then you do not make yourself equal to God, you cannot apprehend God; for like is known by like." [46] And then it immediately tells us just how this may be achieved:

> Leap clear of all that is corporeal, and make yourself grow to a like expanse with that greatness which is beyond all measure; rise above all time, and become eternal; then you will apprehend God. Think that for you too nothing is impossible; deem that you too are immortal, and that you are able to grasp all things in your thought . . . find your home in the haunts of every living creature; make yourself higher than all heights, and lower than all depths; bring together in yourself all opposites of quality, heat and cold, dryness and fluidity; think that you are everywhere at once . . . grasp in your thought all this at once, all times and places, all substances and qualities and magnitudes together; then you can apprehend God. [47]

What is truly striking in this passage are the references to the opposites and how one should bring them together in oneself. It is as if this ancient text was anticipating the employment of the archetype of astrology as a meditational device.

Whereas, as we have attempted suggestively to substantiate, the sidereal zodiac appears to represent sym-

[45] *Ibid.*, Vol. VII: *Two Essays on Analytical Psychology* (London: Routledge & Kegan Paul, 1953), p. 175.
[46] *Corpus Hermeticum*, ed. and trans. by Walter Scott, Vol. I (Oxford, England: Clarendon Press, 1924), p. 221.
[47] *Ibid.*

bolically the effects of the phenomenal world and cosmos on the somatic realm of being, the Ptolemaic or tropical zodiac appears to portray symbolically the compensating activities of the psychic realm. The somatic (sidereal) and the psychic (Ptolemaic) systems are two distinctly different systems, each independent of the other in its operations. That the two mesh at some juncture is apparent and suggests the possibility that the ordering principle encompasses both the psychic and somatic realms. It is akin to the God image so many religions describe as affecting and containing both the somatic and psychic realms of being. "The movement of the Kosmos then, and of every living being that is material, is caused, not by things outside the body, but things within it, which operate outwards from within; that is to say, either by soul or by something else that is incorporeal." [48]

> O nobly-born, these realms are not come from somewhere outside thyself. They come from within the four divisions of thy heart, which, including its centre, make the five directions. They issue from within there, and shine upon thee. . . . The deities, too, are not come from somewhere else: they exist from eternity within the faculties of thine own intellect. Know them to be of that nature. [49]

It is this ground of the psyche, this ordering principle, that is at the heart of the occult arts. In astrology it takes the form of the astrological archetype. As we shall now see, the dynamic and structure of this symbol appear in the Oriental psyche also through the agency of the *I Ching*, or *Book of Changes*.

[48] *Ibid.*, p. 139.
[49] *The Tibetan Book of the Dead*, trans. by W. Y. Evans-Wentz (New York: Oxford University Press, 1960), pp. 121–122.

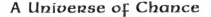

2

A Universe of Chance

Nature says few words.

—*Tao Te Ching*

THE POPULARITY with which the *I Ching* has been received in the West during the past twenty years can only be attributed to the ease of its method. No special knowledge is required, nor is there any need for laborious and time-consuming calculations. The user need only memorize one simple operation and have at his disposal a modicum of credulity. Yet this single work has baffled the minds of the ablest of occultists and philosophers while causing millions throughout the world to stake their lives on its pronouncements. We would not be too far wrong in saying that the *I Ching* has become as popular as astrology and as bestselling a work as the Bible. In fact there is a good chance that more people own the *I Ching* than do the New Testament. This strange set of events would be more than enough reason for us to consider the book. But, as we shall see, there are even stranger reasons.

The *I Ching*, or *Book of Changes* as it is commonly translated, constitutes one of the five Confucian classics, the other four being *The Book of History* (*Shu Ching*), *The Book of Odes* (*Shih Ching*), *The Book of Rites* (*Li*

Chi), and *The Spring and Autumn Annals* (*Ch'un Ch'iu.*) To this list is sometimes added the *Music* (*Yueh*), no longer preserved as a separate work, causing the classics sometimes to be referred to as the six classics. Throughout the course of Chinese history each of the above-mentioned books at one time or another fell into disfavor—with the exception of the *I Ching*, whose origins reach as far back as the twelfth century B.C.

In its divinatory form it appeared sometime around the fourth century B.C. along with two other works entitled *Manifestation of Change in the Mountains* (*Lien Shan*) and *Flow and Return to Womb and Tomb* (*Kuei Ts'ang*). These two earlier texts were to all appearances similar in construction to the present-day *I Ching*.

The *I Ching* as we have it today is composed of sixty-four six-lined configurations of broken and unbroken lines, each figure of which is assigned a specific title with an accompanying text. These figures are called the hexagrams. In addition, each line of a hexagram has assigned to it a cryptic passage accompanied by an explanatory section (The reader unfamiliar with *I Ching* usage will find a small guide in Appendix B.) Originally devised as a fortune-telling device, the book in time became a repository for the finest philosophic speculation on the nature of the universe and man that China could produce. It remains a philosophic work of the first order, a guide to life based on two central principles— the Tao and the yin-yang.

The Tao

Central to all Chinese thought is the idea that there is one underlying motivating principle in the universe called the Tao, a term that has rather loosely been translated into "way," or "road." In order to arrive more closely at a fuller understanding of this concept as it appears in the *I Ching*, it will be necessary first to consider it in the light of its origins.

The only instance in Chinese culture where the supreme coordinating principle of the universe was represented by an anthropomorphic being was in the early Shang dynasty, c. 1600 B.C. Even then the ruler of the universe was not thought of as a being with the features of a man, but simply as *T'ien* ("heaven") or *Ti* ("God"). *Shang Ti* ("supreme emperor") was the supreme authority. Without question the term *Tien* appears more frequently in the writings of the philosophers than *Shang Ti*. The term *T'ien*, however, has a broad range of meaning. The first meaning refers us to its material nature in the form of sky, the actual heavens surrounding the earth. The idea of an anthropomorphic ruling power suggestive of, if not a synonym for, *Shang Ti* is contained in the second meaning. The third finds its equivalent in our concept nature, a dynamic and motivating principle in and of the world. The fourth meaning corresponds to the Chinese concept of fate (*ming*), and the final one refers us to heaven as an ethical stratum from which moral law stems. [1]

All of these meanings for *T'ien* eventually became incorporated in the term "Tao." In its earliest use, Tao simply meant the "way of man," or his conduct as an ethical and socially responsible creature. In this sense

---

[1] See Fung Yu-lan, *A History of Chinese Philosophy*, trans. by Derk Bodde (Princeton, N.J.: Princeton University Press, 1952), Vol. I, pp. 131 ff.

the word referred to the mores of the culture, the realm of strictly human affairs. With the advent of Confucius and his school, the term took on broader philosophic significance.

Confucius was a humanist in that he concerned himself solely with human relations and the teaching of the supreme virtue, *jen*, which has usually been translated as "virtue" or "morality." Confucius, in attempting to explain *jen* to his disciples, said:

> Now the man of perfect virtue, wishing to be established himself, seeks also to establish others; wishing to be enlarged himself, he seeks to enlarge others. To be able to judge of others by what is nigh in ourselves;—this may be called the art of virtue.

> To subdue one's self and return to propriety, is perfect virtue. . . . Look not at what is contrary to propriety; listen not to what is contrary to propriety; speak not what is contrary to propriety; make no movement which is contrary to propriety.[2]

Confucius also believed that in orderly conduct there exists an inherent principle imbued with ethical qualities. If adhered to, this principle would lead to a societal setting in which the interests of people complemented one another. For a prince or a peasant to be aligned with this principle, all he need do is apply propriety and correct conduct to his circumstance:

> Carriages have all wheels of the same size; all writing is with the same characters; and for conduct there are the same rules.

[2] Confucius, *Analects*, VI, 28, and XII, 1, in *The Four Books*, trans. by James Legge (1892).

Only by perfect virtue can the perfect path [Tao], in all its courses, be made a fact.[3]

However, man was not believed to be guided simply by the Tao, but to have an active responsibility toward it: "It is man that can make the Way great and not the Way that can make man great." [4] In addition, the practice of *jen*, the responsibility toward the Tao, and the maintenance of society were all specifically *human* matters. While Confucius did believe in spirits, he felt that they should be respectfully kept at a distance, for ultimately, "If you cannot serve man, how can you know to serve spirits?"

It was with the appearance of the *Tao Te Ching* that the Tao suddenly revealed its metaphysical dimension. The Taoists held that the Tao was the way the universe worked and had nothing to do with proper conduct in society or government. To them the Tao was not something that had to be enhanced by man's actions but rather that which enhanced man when he imitated its operations. To achieve this, one had to give way to the Tao by not doing, by doing only that which was spontaneous and in accord with the needs of the moment. The Tao was not a principle to be manipulated and put to use by society, but rather a power with which each individual should become aligned. It was the order of nature and prime mover behind the entire machinery of the universe regulating every event. Where the Confucian sought to regulate, the Taoist sought to be regulated.

[3] Confucius, *Doctrine of the Mean*, XXVIII, 3, and XXVII, 5, in *The Four Books*.
[4] *The Analects of Confucius*, trans. by Arthur Waley (London: George Allen & Unwin, 1938), p. 142.

When the *I Ching* was set into its final form about the second century of our era, the Confucians responsible for its format had already become greatly influenced by the Taoist concept of the Tao. Because of this the Tao took on yet another dimension of meaning. Whereas the Taoist thought of the Tao as a property that was nameless by virtue of its nonexistence or paraexistence, the Confucians working on the *I Ching* felt that it could not only be named but could actually be identified in things. Everything had its *Tao-ness*, that is, everything contained within it the idea of its own specific function or principle.

The Tao of the *I Ching* takes on the two earlier definitions: It is at one and the same time the moral order of society and the spirit of the universe. To "be in Tao" therefore means to be morally correct as a social being and spiritually in step with the rhythm or pulse of the universe. This pulse in turn expressed the bipolar unity of the Tao in the form of yin and yang.

Yin-Yang

The second concept central to all Chinese thought is that of yin and yang. The terms originally stood for two sides of a mountain, both terms compounded with the character *fou,* "mound of earth." The southern side of the mountain, that which was exposed to sunlight, was called the yang side, while the northern side was entitled the yin. In time these two terms came to be identified with the two pulses of the Tao as it acts in the world—one active, the other quiescent; the first masculine, the second feminine. The masculine pulse, yang, is thought of as active, cold, dry, and creative. The feminine pulse, yin, is thought of as inactive, warm, moist, and receptive.

In the *I Ching* the yang principle receives the notation of an unbroken line; the yin, a broken line. Each hexagram therefore is thought of as a revelation of the operation of the yin and the yang in any given situation.

With the exception of hexagrams 48, The Well, and 50, The Caldron, every hexagram in the *I Ching* refers us to natural phenomena. Because its framers were convinced that the book's sixty-four hexagrams symbolized every possible phase of such phenomena, each hexagram must be thought of as representating a specific "time," the nature of which is given us by the hexagram title. In effect, each hexagram contains within itself the "Taoness" of the phenomena under consideration. Even more important is the suggestion that the natural phenomena are to be analyzed within the context of human experience, for it is just that that the phenomena ultimately affect. Such a phrase as "crossing the great water" would therefore not be taken as an oracular announcement that one should move either his physical body or his home, but that one should arrive at a new attitude, cross over from one point of view to another. A short example of the type of interpretation the *I Ching* demands might be helpful here.

In hexagram 18, Work on What Has Been Spoiled (decay), we are told in two separate instances that we must work on what has been spoiled by the mother and by the father. This does not necessarily refer us to one's actual parents but rather to the qualities of the opposites. To work on what has been spoiled by the mother translates into work on what has been spoiled by too receptive, quiescent, and inactive an attitude or position as would be fostered by the yin. By the same token to work on what has been spoiled by the father translates into modifying too expansive, active, and cold an attitude as would be fostered by the yang.

By being attentive to the interplay of the yin and yang lines in a hexagram, one is witness to the operations of the two primal powers as they evolve in the universe. Because these powers were later identified by the Chinese as forms of psychic energy contained within the individual, what one really experiences in this drama is the activity of the opposites within one's own psyche. In other words, they are operations that occur within the core of our being rather than those that take place in the external world, which in the long run is truly created by our inner condition.

By suggesting that the *I Ching* actually reveals to us the ground of our interiosity, we must be willing to admit to ourselves that a book is capable of revealing to us the nature of our individual condition. There is no escaping it—this is the premise within which all those who employ the *I Ching* must operate. Here it is not a matter of our chemical or glandular systems being affected by meteorological phenomena, sunspots, lunations, or the march of the seasons. The *I Ching* does not operate through these agencies. It simply operates on what appears to be nothing more than a chance occurrence given us by the throwing of three coins. The demands astrology makes on reason appear infinitesimal in comparison with what is asked of us here. However, modern science does appear to have some answers as to how this seemingly impossible situation may be explained. In our attempt to discover how the *I Ching* works, we will have to take a number of detours, the most immediate being one in which it will be necessary to discuss parapsychological phenomena.

The Transmission of ESP

Up until recently the entire matter of extrasensory perception, especially the ability to transmit information from one individual to another without employing any of the known means of communication, was considered some type of intellectual madness, a spot on the white gown of science. Research has since to a considerable degree proved the reality of these phenomena, and several findings appear to shed light in areas not generally investigated by parapsychological researchers—the question of how the *I Ching* could conceivably work, for instance.

Dr. Gertrude Schmeidler, first vice-president of the American Society for Psychical Research and a teacher at The City College of New York, was asked in a recent interview how ESP is transmitted, to which she replied:

> there are just two possibilities to explain how information . . . could be picked up miles away by ESP. One is that there is some unknown kind of energy which carries the information. If this is so, we'd expect the ESP to be much worse when distances were bigger, and this may not be true, as Captain Mitchell's space-earth experiment shows . . . very tentatively I have shifted to the only alternative that I can see: that there isn't an energy beam that carries the information. . . . The second alternative . . . is that it might be through another dimension.[5]

[5] "Dr. Gertrude Schmeidler in Interview," *Psychic*, Vol. III (February, 1972), p. 32.

Dr. Schmeidler referred to the law of causality when she said that if there were some form of energy carrying the information in ESP tests there should be a marked effect on transmission as the distances between sender and receiver grow greater.

The philosophic concept underlying the empirically based research of Western science presupposes the existence of a space-time continuum that is defined by the energy of bodies in motion. Every cause and effect is an expression of the transmission of energy, which in turn reveals the distance between two bodies in terms of time. All causal relationships therefore will be affected by the distance between A and B. The farther B is from A in space, the longer the time period. What Dr. Schmeidler was pointing to is the fact that the transmission of information from one person to another via the channel of ESP should be, according to the law of causality, affected by distance. Yet the fact is that distance in no way seems to affect the transmission and reception of such information. This was established three decades ago by J. B. Rhine at the Parapsychological Laboratories at Duke University.

What Rhine observed was that in the "transmission" of a target by an experimenter concentrating on an image and its reception by another person, a "receiver," time was not affected by distance. No matter how far or how near the two experimenters were in relation to one another, the time factor remained constant. If energy, in the sense we normally think of it in the form of the transmitted image, was present, it was not operating in the field of causality.

Dr. Schmeidler's second proposal, that the transmission of information is taking place through another dimension, was originally suggested by a number of other researchers. Whately Carington proposed in 1945 that such transmissions take place in some subconscious area through the agency of "group minds" contained therein.[6] Professor A. C. Hardy went further and stated that there may be a "sort of species memory governing to some extent the pattern of behaviour of the individuals of a race,"[7] and that individuals might actually therefore communicate with one another through the medium of this field of unconscious memory. In each instance the suggestion put forward was that human beings share a group mind, or unconscious. Although Dr. Schmeidler did not speak of this other dimension as a property of psyche, the implication is there.

Of course we also find statements concerning the existence of a shared mind long before parapsychological research emerged. In the Sanskrit "Lankavatra Scripture" we find:

> Universal Mind is like a great ocean, its surface ruffled by waves and surges but its depths remaining forever unmoved. In itself it is devoid of personality and all that belongs to it, but by reason of the defilement upon its face it is like an actor and plays a variety of parts, among which a mutual functioning takes place and the mind-system arises. The principle of intellection becomes divided and mind, the functions of mind, . . . take on individuation. The sevenfold gradation of mind appears: namely, intuitive self-realisation, thinking-desiring-discriminating, seeing, hearing, tasting, smelling, touching, and all their interactions and reactions take their rise. . . .

[6] Whately Carington, *Telepathy* (London: Methuen, 1945).
[7] A. C. Hardy, "Telepathy and Evolutionary Theory," *Journal of the American Society for Psychical Research,* May, 1950.

> Thus Universal Mind becomes the storage and clearing house of all the accumulated products of mentation and action since beginningless time.[8]

What is interesting here is the idea that this larger universal mind gives birth to a smaller and limited mind.

Turning briefly to the Chinese philosopher Chu Hsi, we find a similar statement about the existence of a universal mind:

> The principle of the mind is the Great Ultimate. The activity and tranquility of the mind are the yin and yang. . . . Fundamentally there is only one Great Ultimate, yet each of the myriad things has been endowed with it and each in itself possesses the Great Ultimate in its entirety. . . . [It] has neither spatial restriction nor physical form or body. There is no spot where it may be placed. . . . While the state before activity begins cannot be spoken of as the Great Ultimate, nevertheless the Principles of pleasure, anger, sorrow, and joy are already inherent in it. Pleasure and joy belong to yang and anger and sorrow belong to yin.[9]

Here too we are presented with the idea of a universal mind underlying man's individual psyche. But more important is the statement that the Great Ultimate has "neither spatial restriction nor physical form or body. There is no spot where it may be placed." This appears to answer the description, in somewhat negative terms,

---

[8] Dwight Goddard, ed., *A Buddhist Bible* (Thetford, Vt.: Dwight Goddard, 1938), p. 306.

[9] Wing-Tsit Chan, ed. and trans., *A Source Book in Chinese Philosophy* (Princeton, N.J.: Princeton University Press, 1969), pp. 628 ff.

of what Dr. Schmeidler's "other dimension" would have to be: It could not be located in the space-time continuum, bound neither by space nor by time.

Some twenty years ago Dr. C. G. Jung commented on the nature of this other dimension and its operations:

> The "absolute knowledge" which is characteristic of synchronistic phenomena, a knowledge not mediated by the sense organs, supports the hypothesis of a self-subsistent meaning, or even expresses its existence. Such a form of existence can only be transcendental, since, as the knowledge of future or spatially distant events shows, it is contained in a psychically relative space and time, that is to say, in an irrepresentable space-time continuum.[10]

Jung surmised that because no observable evidence of transmission could be discovered in the Rhine experiments, the information arose within the psyche of the recipient himself. That is, the images "transmitted" by one individual were being directly experienced in the psyche of another. This was a bizarre suggestion to accept. In order to understand how such a phenomenon might work, it is necessary briefly to discuss Jung's theory of the collective unconscious, or *objective psyche* as it is commonly called.

The Objective Psyche

If we follow to its logical conclusion, Freud's thesis that the unconscious is essentially a repository for re-

[10] C. G. Jung, *The Collected Works of C. G. Jung*, ed. by G. Adler, M. Fordham, H. Read, and W. McGuire, trans. by R. F. C. Hull, Vol. VIII: *The Structure and Dynamics of the Psyche* (London: Routledge & Kegan Paul, 1960), p. 506.

pressed material that at one time was conscious, a tab-
ula rasa upon which we transcribe our sins, we might
reason that with little more than hard work we should
be capable of emptying the unconscious. Having re-
trieved all that was once reprehensible and repressed,
we would therefore no longer dream, and if we did, at
least our dreams would no longer contain burdensome
symbols expressive of our "problems," since there would
no longer be any. What Jung noticed during the successful course of an analysis and its satisfactory conclusion along personalistic lines was that his patients did
not stop dreaming. They not only continued to dream,
but the material of their dreams took on a far different
and impersonal quality. Their dreams were filled with
what Jung later came to call archetypes.

> The archetypes do not represent anything external,
> non-psychic, although they do of course owe the
> concreteness of their imagery to impressions re-
> ceived from without. Rather, independently of, and
> sometimes in direct contrast to, the outward forms
> they may take, they represent the life and essence
> of a non-individual psyche. Although this psyche is
> innate in every individual it can neither be modified
> nor possessed by him personally.[11]

The collective unconscious and its archetypes therefore represent a symbol-producing realm, the archetypes
being "the pictorial forms of the instincts, for the unconscious reveals itself to the conscious mind in images." [12]

---

[11] *Ibid.*, Vol. XVI: *The Practice of Psychotherapy* (London: Routledge & Kegan Paul, 1954), p. 169.
[12] Erich Neumann, *The Origins and History of Consciousness*
(New York: Pantheon Books, 1964), p. xv.

The entire process is simply a matter of nonspecific energic impulses becoming anthropomorphized.

> These "primoridal images," which are similar only in their underlying pattern, are based on a principle of form that has always been inherent in the psyche: they are "inherited" only in the sense that the structure of the psyche . . . embodies a universally human heritage, and bears within it a faculty of manifesting itself in definite and specific forms . . . they are the "primordial pattern" underlying the *invisible order* of the unconscious psyche.[13]

For every instinctual type of response there is a corresponding image based on the structural dynamic of the impulse. Thus, the basic instinct behind gestation, nurturing, and all other activities one may associate with mothering gave birth to the image of the great mother in ancient religions. The degree to which the personified energy of an instinct may be taken to represent a cosmic and exterior force is best illustrated by the Vedic figure Hiranyagarbha:

> There was nothing whatsoever here in the beginning. It was covered only by Death (Hiranyagarbha), or Hunger, for hunger is death. He created the mind, thinking, "Let me have a mind." . . . He desired, "Let me have a second form (body)." He, death or Hunger, brought about the union of speech (the *Vedas*) with the mind.[14]

Here the instinct hunger takes on cosmic proportions to become the devouring universal mind, the ordering

[13] Jolan Jacobi, *Complex/Archetype/Symbol* (New York: Pantheon Books, 1959), pp. 51–52.
[14] *The Brhadaranyaka Upanishad*, trans. by Swami Madhavananda (Calcutta: Advaita Ahsrama, 1965), pp. 15 and 29.

principle of the universe that brings things to being out of an instinctual need. This was the nature of the material Jung's patients began to produce in their psyches once they had satisfactorily dealt with the personal ground of their experience: archetypal symbolism of an impersonal character, more akin to myth.

A pictorial representation of the objective psyche and its relation to the individual psyches might look something like Figure 6. The unshaded portions of the individual psyches represent the conscious sphere; the shaded, the personal unconscious. All of them are grounded, as it were, in the larger sphere they all share —the objective psyche in which the archetypes reside, here represented by the asterisks. It would not be going too far afield in thinking of the objective psyche as a fluid field in which the archetypes have free movement.

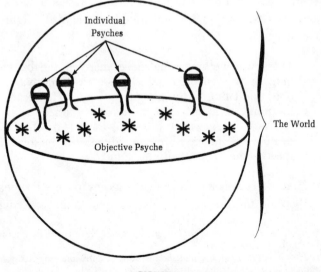

FIGURE 6

This concept of a "great ocean of knowledge" is not unfamiliar to a number of philosophies and religions.

In neo-Confucian philosophy we also find a statement about the archetypes, called *li* ("principles")[15] in Chinese: "All things in the world may be understood through Principle [*li*]. There being a thing, there must also be a pattern for it. Each individual thing must have its individual Principle." [16]

And yet another neo-Confucian tells us,

> What fills the universe is but molds and forms (copies). With our insight (or clarity of mind), the system and principles of the universe cannot be examined. When there are physical forms, one may trace back to the cause of that which is hidden, and when there is no physical form, one may trace back to the cause of that which is manifested.[17]

And finally, "In an examination of the Tao we find the ten thousand *li* all there complete." This refers us to the idea that the *li*, or archetypes in our terminology, are contained in the Tao, or objective psyche.

We have presented material above, indicating that the Tao is an aspect of mind contained in man himself, suggesting that it corresponds to Jung's objective psyche. This idea is nowhere so clearly stated as by Lu Chiu-yüan, a contemporary of Chu Hsi: "The ten thousand things [18] are profusely contained within a square inch of

---

[15] "As used in Neo-Confucianism, *li* is a designation for the immaterial and metaphysical principle or principles that underlie, yet transcend, the physical universe" (Yu-lan, *A History of Chinese Philosophy*, Vol. II, p. 444).

[16] *Ibid.*, p. 503.

[17] Chan, *A Source Book in Chinese Philosophy*, p. 503.

[18] The term "ten thousand things" is a Chinese synonym for all things in the world.

space (i.e., the mind). Filling the mind and, pouring forth, filling the entire universe . . . there is nothing that is not this Principle (*li*)."[19] Fung Yu-lan, commenting on an earlier quote by this philosopher, noted that according to Chiu-yüan the Tao is nothing other than the mind. If the Tao is "the hidden reservoir of all things" and at the same time is compared to the mind of humans, what is being referred to is an aspect of mind that is not only all-encompassing, comparable to the "ten thousand things," but in no way limited in the manner of ego-consciousness. The Chinese sage refers to the Tao-mind as "something undefined and yet complete in itself, Born before Heaven-and-Earth. Silent and boundless, Standing alone without change, Yet pervading all without fail."[20] When this Tao-mind is contained within man as well, it cannot help but be analogous to Jung's formulation of the objective psyche.

Other material exists that suggests that the Tao of Chinese philosophy, which we find in *I Ching,* and the objective psyche are of the same cloth. The reader is asked to understand the similarities between the Tao and the objective psyche, or field of immediate knowledge, from the material presented above as philosophic and psychological classifications of a principle residing beneath every individual's psychic system. The Tao, which we now know as synonymous with the objective psyche, might therefore be the "within" through which the transmission of ESP experiments take place.

[19] Yu-lan, *A History of Chinese Philosophy,* Vol. II, p. 574.
[20] *The Tao Te Ching,* trans. by John C. H. Wu (New York: St. John's University Press, 1961), pp. 33–35.

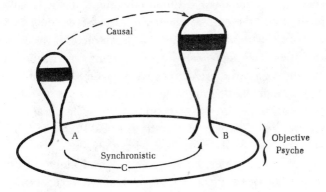

FIGURE 7

In Figure 7 let us assume that the transmitter (A) is in London, and that the receiver (B) is in New York. According to the Rhine experiments, and others that have since followed, the causal connection that logically should have been present in the space-time continuum was not present. We might say, then, that the manner in which the information was transmitted, according to Jung's ideas, was through the ground of immediate experience, or the objective psyche, experienced as an interior event.

Somehow, in a manner not yet understood or appreciated, this field of immediate experience is brought to play in parapsychological and synchronistic events. It is as if the transmitted material from one person strikes the chord of a corresponding structural form or archetype $(C$ in our diagram) in the objective psyche, causing its echo or resonance to be "heard" by the person waiting to receive the message.

Having already equated the objective psyche or field of immediate experience with the Tao of the *I Ching*, we might extrapolate further that the structural forms or archetypes are represented by the hexagrams. Earlier in our discussion the archetypes were pictured (Figure 7) indiscriminately floating within the field of the objective psyche. This is in strong contrast to the hexagrams of the *I Ching*, which delineate the field of the Tao. Whereas in the Occidental model the objective psyche is viewed without boundaries or limits, the Chinese model states that these limits are known and portrayed by the hexagrams. Not only are the boundaries of the individual psyche known in this latter model, but the boundaries of the objective psyche or the Tao are known as well. The sixty-four hexagrams of the *I Ching* therefore become a statement from the psyche about its own structure.

> The Book of Changes contains the measure of heaven and earth; therefore it enables us to comprehend the tao of heaven and earth and its order....
> Since in this way man comes to resemble heaven and earth, he is not in conflict with them. His wisdom embraces all things, and his tao brings order into the whole world; therefore he does not err. . . .
> He rejoices in heaven and has knowledge of his fate, therefore he is free of care. . . .
> In it are included the forms and the scope of everything in the heavens and on earth, so that nothing escapes it. In it all things everywhere are completed, so that none is missing.[21]

[21] *The I Ching or Book of Changes,* the Richard Wilhelm translation, trans. into English by Cary F. Baynes (New York: Pantheon, 1955), Vol. I, pp. 315 ff.

When employing the book, the inquirer becomes both his own transmitter and receiver. The answer to his question comes from the depths of his own psyche and finds correspondence in the sixty-four hexagrams set out in the *Book of Changes*. The statement that the *I Ching* makes about itself, therefore, is that through the sixty-four delineations, which are representative of all possible human events, it reveals the workings of the objective psyche as a formulating principle in the world in its capacity as the common ground of experience. In other

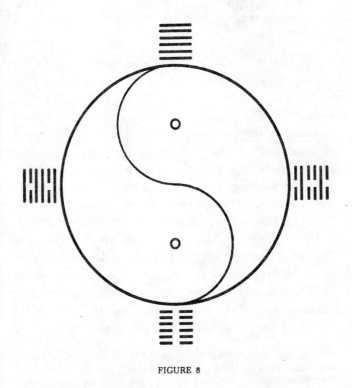

FIGURE 8

words, the book presents itself as a model of the substratum of the human psyche, as the symbolic representation of a living principle at the base of the universe. The dynamics behind this relationship between the microcosm and the macrocosm were seen by the Nobel prize–winning physicist Wolfgang Pauli, when he wrote:

> The process of understanding nature as well as the happiness that man feels in understanding, that is, in the conscious realization of new knowledge, seems thus to be based on a correspondence, a "matching" of inner images preexistent in the human psyche with external objects and their behaviour.[22]

Whereas in sidereal astrology we were faced, on the one hand, with man's relationship with meteorological phenomena, and on the other, in the Ptolemaic zodiac, with a symbolic presentation of the underlying structure or order of the psychological and physiological aspects of man, in the *I Ching* we find a philosophic construct of the psychological ground underlying both these systems. Each hexagram is representative of a class of objects or states of being in time. The time exemplified by the hexagram is of a generalized nature and refers us to the principle (the Tao) underlying all the objects or characteristics of the time related to that class. Hexagram 32, Duration, therefore, refers to different phases of duration and the ensuing effects of their possible combinations. These combinations are given us by the changing lines one might receive. While the "Tao" of

22 Wolfgang Pauli, "The Influence of Archetypal Ideas on the Scientific Ideas of Kepler," in C. G. Jung and Wolfgang Pauli, *The Interpretation of Nature and the Psyche* (New York: Bollingen Series, Vol. LI, 1955), p. 152.

Duration could then be understood as a *li* or achetypal configuration underlying all concepts of duration, the hexagram as a unit reveals the nature of the Tao of the moment, the underlying principle active in the moment; and each of the lines refers to the parts that go to make up that whole. *The Great Commentary,* an appendix to the *I Ching,* tells us: "Circumstances follow distinct tendencies, each in accordance with its nature. All things are made distinct from one another by the definitiveness of their classes. . . . Phenomena take form in heaven; shapes take form on earth." The hexagrams, then, are symbolic of tendencies, nonspecific forces or powers originating in "heaven" or the objective psyche, which in turn give birth to "circumstances," the "shapes" that take form on earth. The idea behind each hexagram reveals a highly sophisticated inquiry into the nature of the universe and its effect on man.

It should by now be apparent that both astrology and the *I Ching* operate from common ground, and that these two distinctive systems offer us two different views of what this field of immediate knowledge or objective psyche looks like.

Astrology purports to reveal the operations of what must ultimately be considered a mechanistic view of the universe. True, much of traditional astrology relates to the activity of spirit and soul, but it speaks of them within the context of a complex system of mechanical operations of predictable phenomena. The operations themselves are thought of as visible in that they are synonymous with the movements of the planets. In the *I Ching,* on the other hand, we are presented with operations further removed from the observable universe. The *I Ching* deals with the truly invisible, defining qualities of time by the operations of metaphysical forces, the yin and the yang. In its operations it reveals to us aspects of the field of immediate knowledge at its periphery. Astrology speaks of that which is closest to man; the *I Ching*, that which is farthest from him. It is in the *I Ching* that we may find philosophic confirmation of the phenomena of sensory receptors that lie beyond the range of consciousness, receptors that have been revealed to us through scientific research and through the symbolic patterning of the Ptolemaic universe, as we discussed in the last chapter. The *I Ching*'s diagrams of

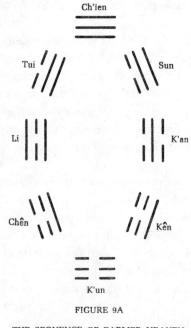

FIGURE 9A

THE SEQUENCE OF EARLIER HEAVEN,
OR PRIMAL ARRANGEMENT

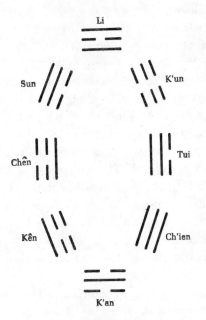

FIGURE 9B

THE SEQUENCE OF LATER HEAVEN,
OR INNER-WORLD ARRANGEMENT

earlier and later heaven are particularly revealing for the purposes of this discussion. These two diagrams are thought to contain all the knowledge of the universe.[23]

In Figure 9A, "The Sequence of Earlier Heaven, or Primal Arrangement," we find the trigrams portrayed in their polar relationships, each trigram balanced and complementing its opposite. The text appended to this

[23] The early framers of the *I Ching* thought of the diagram of earlier heaven as being beneath and shining through the diagram of later heaven, yielding yet further permutations of the trigrams.

diagram tells us, "Counting that which is going into the past depends on the forward movement. Knowing that which is to come depends on the backward movement." [24]

The movement referred to here is that of the trigrams as they become manifest in the universe. The statement that one can come to know either the past or the future by attending to the movements of these trigrams clearly points to the idea of a space-time continuum beyond reality as we know it. The dimension of this domain must be considered cosmic; and the diagram, an attempt to define its operations through the agency of eight primal potencies inherent in natural phenomena. The placement of the trigrams in complementary positions reminds one of the signs in the astrological archetype, which also share this feature.

Figure 9B, "The Sequence of Later Heaven, or Inner-World Arrangement," presents the trigrams in serial form within the context of temporal progressions in the phenomenal world. Not only do they portray the unfolding of the year, but the hours of the day as well, each trigram representing a three-hour period.

The diagram of earlier heaven complements the archetype of the zodiac, whereas the diagram of later heaven in its depiction of earthly events complements the house system in Ptolemaic astrology. To understand the significance of the two diagrams under discussion, however, they must be approached as expressions of energy. That they specifically refer us to the manifestation of energy is apparent from the trigrams' very operations as phenomena of the cosmos on the one hand, and nature on the other. The two diagrams are simply models

[24] *I Ching*, Vol. I, p. 285.

of the Tao, or great ultimate as it was later called, in manifestation on two planes.

We can also see that each diagram possesses features that correspond to those of a mandala. The depiction of the union of opposites, symbolization of cosmic and temporal space, a structural component based on the number 3, are only a few of the mandalic aspects we discussed in Chapter 1. The astrological achetype also conformed to this definition, and like one of the three types of mandalas was a spontaneous product of the collective mind prompted by a conflict or crisis. We recognize the mandala as a symbolic representation of an ordering principle that Jung termed the self—an archetype representing the totality of the psyche, including its personal and collective aspects. The diagrams of earlier and later heaven, inasmuch as they are further differentiations of the concept Tao, appear to be representations of the Oriental self.

The Birth of the Collective Mandala

Arnold Toynbee proposed that God allows man to be challenged so that in man's response to the challenge he may come to realize the creative realm of existence:

> The single ordeals of Job and Faust represent, in the intuitive language of fiction, the infinitely multiple ordeal of man; and in the language of theology, the same vast consequence is represented as following from the superhuman encounters that are portrayed in the Book of Genesis and in the New Testament. . . . By the light of Mythology, we have gained some insight into the nature of challenges and responses. We have come to see that creation is the outcome of an encounter, or to re-translate the

imagery of myths into the terminology of Science—
that genesis is a function of interaction.[25]

The challenges, Toynbee goes on to explain in long and
detailed analysis, can come from either the social environment or the natural environment. He implies that
only one of the two challenges is necessary to manifest a
starting point for a civilization. Since we find that in the
Oriental's experience both challenges (social and environmental) had to be met, it appears that the challenges
proposed by Toynbee must not be singular events in a
culture. The manifestation of one challenge does not
preclude the appearance of the other. Both forms of en-
counter, then, are inevitable for the maintenance and
continuance of a group. Here we do not mean to challenge the theories of so erudite an historian and scholar
as Arnold Toynbee, but only to suggest that the failure
of civilizations may have something to do with their ina-
bility to either recognize or meet a second challenge.
The group, however, may act in much the same way as
an individual personality and may disregard the psyche's
demand to meet reality through avenues distinctively
foreign to its previously successful approaches, an attitude that inevitably leads to stagnation.

Whichever the sphere from which the challenge
comes, according to Toynbee, in order for the challenge

[25] Arnold J. Toynbee, *A Study of History* (New York: Oxford
University Press, 1962), Vol. I, pp. 274 and 299. Borrowing the
term "yin," symbolic of rest in its positive sense, sloth in its negative, Toynbee states that God allows adverse circumstances to
challenge man out of the negative phase of yin. In so doing He
causes man to pass over into the positive phase of yang, the creative and active state of the universe, which leads to the flowering
of civilization.

to be experienced as an impetus toward action, it must be met by the creative minority of the civilization in question, and be met with "self-determination" if the group is to continue to exist. The key phrase here is "self-determination." Another historian, P. A. Means, has written:

> Environment. . . is not the total causation in culture-shaping. . . . It is, beyond doubt, the most conspicuous single factor. . . . But there is still an indefinable factor which may best be designated quite frankly as x, the unknown quantity, apparently psychological in kind.[26]

The indefinable factor that Means feels to be psychological is obviously the self-determination of the creative minority group to which Toynbee refers. But the phrase "self-determination" only defines the feeling-tone of those individuals. Ostensibly it tells us *how* certain individuals respond to a challenge but not *why*. One begins to find out why, by viewing such self-determination as an expression of the self's attempt to maintain its integrity and continue its development at the evolutionary and collective level. The success of this attempt is signaled by the emergence of a mandala around which all collective values eventually form.

In the period of Chinese history preceding the emergence of the *I Ching* we find the Chinese facing two challenges from God. The first challenge was from the physical environment; the second, from the social environment. The nature of the physical challenge was so

[26] P. A. Means, *Ancient Civilization of the Andes* (New York, 1931), pp. 25–26.

severe and so pervasive it left an indelible imprint on Chinese thought. The environmental challenge has been carefully reconstructed for us by the historian Gaston Maspero:

> It was probably in the great plain of the North-East . . . that the Chinese began to develop their civilization. . . . The climate of this region was extremely severe. . . . The rivers . . . thawed rapidly at the first fine weather and became torrents. . . . The great artery, the Yellow River, with its rapids and sandbanks, is dangerous to navigate; . . . This was the country which was called the Nine Rivers, because it was said, the Yellow River had there nine principal branches. . . . Each year the floods changed the river's course and sought new channels; the shallows became water-logged and turned into great swamps. . . . They were surrounded by belts, varying in width, of land which was too wet for agriculture. . . . The best lands were protected against floods by dykes. . . . The process had been long and cruel. Dykes had to be built against the floods, canals had to be dug to drain the swamps and turn them into dry land. All these works were so ancient that the memory of them was lost in the fog of legend.[27]

The legend that Maspero refers to is that given us in *The Book of History* (*Shu Ching*), where we are told of a great inundation. Called upon to correct the mishap, the legendary hero Yu divided the land into nine portions and was thereby granted by heaven the great plan of the nine classifications. We must assume that it was

[27] Gaston Maspero, quoted in Toynbee, *A Study of History*, Vol. I, pp. 319–320.

this environmental challenge in the form of some ancient deluge to which the symbolism of Chinese philosophy owes its debt.

Out of this time of troubles the first delineation of the Oriental's self was made through the agency of the nine-fold mandala. The self appropriated its symbolic language from the inevitable response to an environmental challenge in the form of flooding—the partitioning of lands around the nine tributaries of the Yellow River. This nine-fold demarcation led to a second delineation, the locating of a sacred center in a structure known as the *ming t'ang*, or "hall of light," reflective not only of the order of the cosmos but also of the affinity between the supreme principle, the Tao, and the Divine King. The third significant expression of this structural motif arising out of the self's activity at the collective level occurred during the feudal period. This was the establishment of the *ching t'ien*, or "well-field system." This system was one in which all land was divided into large squares, each large square subdivided into nine squares. The center square contained the overlord's home and the well used by the adjoining eight families. The philosopher Tung Chung-shu (c. 179–c. 104 B.C.) has left us this description:

> A square *li* [about a third of a mile] comprises one "well" [square], and such a "well" comprises 900 *mou* [Chinese acres], on which the population is settled. A square *li* contains eight families, each having 100 *mou*, whereby (at the minimum) it may feed five persons.[28]

[28] Quoted in Yu-lan, *A History of Chinese Philosophy*, Vol. II, p. 54.

The fourth expression of this mandalic structure was called the diagrams of earlier and later heaven, bearing symbolic and ethical qualities in the form of the *I Ching's* trigrams. In this fourth and further differentiation of the original mandalic motif, the self expresses itself as a metaphysical and philosophical structure.

The second ordeal facing Chinese civilization was, in this case, social. Out of this final challenge of God's came the series of meaningful and so-called accidental events that led to the *I Ching's* creation. Finally, the development of this mandalic structure eventually led to the later Taoist statements to the effect that the human psyche is composed of nine compartments patterned after the well-field system.

In all, there is a two-fold development of this mandalic motif. The first occurred in response to an environmental challenge that led to the structure of Chinese society itself; the second came about in response to the social challenge emerging out of the period of the warring states. This latter challenge resulted in the splintering of the original unit of the naturalistic philosophy indigenous to Chinese culture into the so-called one hundred philosophic schools. The philosophic dimension of Chinese culture was born out of this crisis and is the signal event that speaks of a culture's movement out of the magical dimension, through the *participation mystique* of the group, and toward structures that at least contain the potential for individual expression and development. In this particular instance the potential is contained in the final structure born out of that period, the *I Ching*.

The mandalas of earlier and later heavens symbolize the endeavor on the part of the self, operating at the collective level, to reorganize the splintered portions of Chinese culture over the course of several centuries. By the same token the creation of the archetypal figure of Western astrology might be understood as an attempt on the part of the self to stabilize the events centering around the birth of Christianity and all the social upheaval that it entailed, the transition of Western culture from the Middle East to the West, and the fall of Rome as both a religious and political world power.

As with the astrological archetype, the mandalas of the *I Ching* also symbolize the divine *anthropos*, for the trigrams composing them represent different portions of a human body composed of feminine and masculine attributes. (See Appendix B.)

The Language of Mandalas

If mandalas, as we have suggested, are symbolic statements made by the ordering principle about its operations through the agency of the human psyche, we should expect to find a discernible pattern of operation symbolic of a psychic event. We can test the veracity of our suggestion by analyzing at least one of the *I Ching*'s mandalas. Because the operation of the ordering principle supposedly operates at both the cosmic and temporal levels, the logical choice of diagrams for our analysis would be the diagram of earlier heaven. In an appendix to the *I Ching*, the eight trigrams of this diagram figure prominently in a creation myth. The *I Ching* tells us that the first four trigrams symbolize the activity of the spirit Tao at the cosmic level, the last four the activity of this same spirit during the course of a year at the temporal level. The first trigram, we shall see, symbolizes birth; the last, a completion. If we take the movement of the first four trigrams as symbolic of events occurring at the periphery of the world, beyond conscious observation, eternal and immutable, we could think of them as symbolic of psychic energy operating beyond the realm of consciousness, at the unconscious level. The movements of the last four trigrams, described as representative of operations occurring in the world, as visible and immediately discernible operations, might therefore be thought of as psychic energy operating within the field of ego-consciousness. The transition of the spirit Tao from the cosmic to the mundane level might for our purposes symbolize the transition of energy from the unconscious into the conscious sphere. Because the mandala discribes a creation myth, we may also assume that the "created thing" that passes from the unconscious to consciousness is a "new" quantum of psychic energy never before perceived by man. A newly perceived *idea* would be the best example of such emerging energy.

The *I Ching* tells us that the first trigram to express itself in creation is *Chên*, "thunder." The creation of the world by sound, be it organized as in language or disorganized as in thunder, is a familiar symbol in mythology. So too is the idea that this activity occurs in spring, which the trigram *Chên* symbolizes. In addition this trigram has as one of its major symbolic attributes the image of a seed and for this reason is often given the appellation Beginnings. Within the psychological frame that we established this trigram would symbolize the appearance of the seed of an idea, as yet formless, deep within the unconscious, nothing more than a reverberation.

According to our Chinese text, this reverberation of the spirit then gives rise to the wind that will immediately serve to dissolve the ice of the unformed universe. Again, we find correspondence to those creation myths wherein the active principle of creation is symbolized by a spiritualized wind. Psychologically speaking, the wind may be interpreted by the conscious ego's intuition of an event as yet invisible, within the unconscious—a feeling of expectancy. We cannot yet see the idea, but the effect of its presence, like the wind, is briefly felt, symbolized in the second trigram, *Sun.*

The dissolving of the ice in our creation myth then gives birth to the trigram *K'an,* "water." The major symbolic significations of this trigram are the heart, the blood, and the emotions. The blood, home of the soul, and the heart both strongly suggest the idea of *feeling,* or an emotional response. Within the frame of our psychological model, this third movement of the spirit Tao as psychic energy might symbolize the agitation experienced just before an idea is fully realized. Here the melting of the ice might be likened to the removal of that which has been blocking an idea from passing over into consciousness. A "fluid" condition has transpired, giving birth to an emotional reaction. In addition to the symbols mentioned above, *K'an* also represents the human ear. This is only fitting, since it is at just such a moment during the birth of an idea that one suddenly turns his attention away from the outer world to the inner, listening as it were to what is happening within. Still, the idea is not yet visible.

Out of the preceding moment is born the trigram *Li,* "fire," whose major symbolic attributes are the sun, light, and the eye. All three images are apt symbols for consciousness. With the appearance of this fourth trigram, the activity of the spirit Tao at the cosmic level draws to a close. Here, the idea has appeared at the threshold where it may be perceived by consciousness as symbolized by the light and the human eye.

The next trigram, the first of the four symbolizing the activity of the spirit Tao within the area of consciousness, is *Kên*, "mountain," whose title is Keeping Still. This trigram's symbolic attributes are an entranceway, guardian dogs, the hand, and the fingers. Admittedly, the appearance of a fresh idea on the threshold of consciousness is a delicate thing. At any moment, unless given attention, it can slip back into the darkness of the unconscious. This trigram might therefore symbolize the moment when the idea that appears at the door of consciousness is taken hold of by an attentive ego and guarded against the possibility of its slipping away. One must literally keep one's thoughts still so that attention may be given to the newly emerged idea. Another important attribution of this trigram is that of death and rebirth. Psychologically speaking, the moment outlined here symbolizes the death of one phase of psychic activity and the birth of another—the death phase being unconscious; the rebirth, conscious. *Kên* also symbolizes a large ripe fruit. What began as a seed deep within the unconscious in the symbol of *Chên*, "thunder," has grown into a large fruit ready to be picked. The gestation and maturation process that the seed had to undergo is complete and ready for the harvest of consciousness.

The next trigram, *Tui*, symbolizes the harvest and the mouth. The idea, then, has been picked from the tree of the unconscious and tasted for its worth. *Ch'ien*, the creative, is the next trigram and symbolizes the head, the father, and spirit. This trigram would represent the discriminating creative aspect of Logos, the intellectual machinery that comes into play when one first begins to shape the many aspects of a new idea.

Finally, the last trigram, *K'un,* representing the mother, form, and earth, brings to a close the activity of the energy we have diagramed. The final process in the cycle of an idea is the assigning of a specific form by which it may be grasped. Here the idea is given substance in order to become a permanent feature of consciousness.

The point of the journey we have just taken is to show that the mandala is a symbol that causes us to *experience* meaning and order if we turn our attention to it. In other words, there is something about the nature of our psyches that forces us to seek out order and in so doing creates symbols that engage us in the search.

These symbols, however, are not artificial cultural constructs. They are a part of the underlying philosophic structure of the *I Ching* and as in astrology are based on a quarternity, a trinity, a duality, and a unity. We have already reviewed the latter two structures in our discussion of the yin-yang theory and the Tao. The quarternal structure, reflected in the qualities of the elements in astrology, corresponds roughly to the five elements of Oriental philosophy—fire, water, metal, wood, and earth. Earth is like Aristotle's fifth element, only in that it too is thought of as parent to the other four.

In Figure 10 we find the original unity located at the bottom. The first tier depicts the opposites, yin and yang, immediately after their separation from the Tao. These two principles then divide into the second tier. The creation of the second tier symbolically constitutes

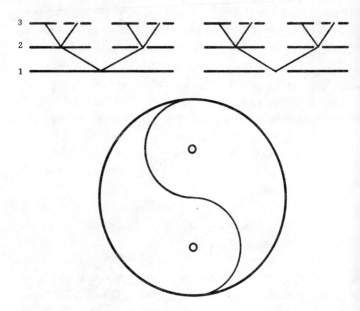

FIGURE 10

the creation of the elements. By combining the lines of the second tier with their "parents" in the first, we arrive at four figures known as greater (☰) and lesser (☱) yang, and greater (☳) and lesser (☷) yin. It is from these four elements that the eight trigrams are born. Because the trigrams constitute the superstructure of nature, we are again witness to the statement that the existence of the world is independent upon the activity of the elements.

The trinitarian structure in the *I Ching* is referred to in one of its appendices, *The Great Commentary*, where it is stated that the six lines of a hexagram represent the way of three powers: the power of earth, the power of man, and the power of heaven. These three primal powers are aspects of one spirit—the spirit Tao, which penetrates the places of heaven, earth, and man to express its specific qualities. Keeping in mind that the hexagram also represents the human body, each hexagram is in essence a macro-microscosmic structure.

Again appears the archetypal structure of the human psyche with its temporal and transpersonal elements. And again the dynamic principle of this entire system is expressed in terms of spirit or energy. What is unusual about this energy is that it too operates within the confines of a specific law.

The Mechanics of Spirit

J. B. Rhine's parapsychological experiments, which we discussed earlier, revealed the absence of any causal factors, specifically energy, in the transmission of ESP. This led to the view that the transmission was an interiorized event. What we did not consider at that time was the possibility that, interiorized or not, the event was one in which some kind of energy still figured. But because of its field of activity the quality of energy would have to be called "psychic." We shall not dwell upon the many theories of psychic energy, since all we need do here is state that the dynamism of psychic systems, both conscious and unconscious, is now almost without exception spoken of in terms of energy.

> the analogy between psychological and physical energy has only a relative validity, for we cannot demonstrate a visible or tangible body of the psyche distinct from the energy inhering in it. But in the realm of physics also, where our hands and eyes tell us there is a solid body, our intellects are faced

with the paradox that this so solid-seeming body may be nothing more than a form of energy; thus it is more than likely that the psyche too is only a form of energy. . . . Just as the manifest energy of physical bodies is only a small part of their total store, so too only a small part of the energy residing in the psyche is at the disposition of the conscious ego and under the control of the personal I. The larger part of physical energy is locked up inside the atoms, and the larger part of the psychic energy is similarly locked up in the instincts, the patterns or forms of biological behaviour, and in the archetypes, the patterns or forms of psychic behaviour.[29]

We also know now that this energy expresses its organization or disorganization in seemingly disparate modes, the most beguiling of which is the symbolic mode most commonly experienced in dreams and fantasies. This tendency of the psychic portion of man to express itself in symbols does not end here but extends itself into such areas as religion, philosophy, mysticism, art, and of special significance for our inquiry, the occult.

In the two arts we have briefly discussed we have seen how this energy manifests itself in symbolic form on the mundane plane. In both systems it is suggested that there is a prime source and operation standing behind these phenomena. Astrology itself does not take any fully rounded philosophic stand on the nature of this source, whereas the *I Ching* does refer us back to the philosophic concept of the Tao, a primal power standing before the world that is inexhaustible and beyond man's conscious realization. The manner in which

[29] M. Esther Harding, *Psychic Energy: Its Source and Transformation* (New York: Pantheon Books, 1963), p. 362.

it is made manifest in the world is explained to us in terms of the polarities of the yin and the yang, about which there has been much speculation. As for the Tao itself, little is told us about *its* internal operations. That it is a plenum of energy is implied throughout the course of Chinese philosophy. In astrology we find the energy broken down into specific modes of activity in the character of the planets, but there too we fail to find mention of the nature of the energy source.

Chinese philosophy does give us a clue by referring to the Tao as mind and to the yin and the yang as its operations. This led to our assumption that the Tao is the objective psyche, or ground of immediate experience, and that the operations of the yin and the yang display the characteristics of the human psyche's dynamism. In those few instances where the interior operation of these two systems are referred to, we find them described in terms of number: "Heaven is one, earth is two; heaven is three, earth four; heaven is five, earth six; heaven is seven, earth eight; heaven is nine, earth ten." [30]

To this we must add Shao Yung's (A.D. 1011–1077) observations:

> By its very nature, the Great Ultimate is unmoved. When it is aroused, it becomes spirit. Spirit leads to number. Number leads to form. Form leads to concrete things. Concrete things undergo infinite transformations, but underlying them is spirit to which they must be resolved. [31]

The *I Ching* is diagrammatic of what the Chinese believed were the boundaries of the Tao, or the supreme

[30] *I Ching*, Vol. I, p. 331.
[31] Chan, *A Source Book in Chinese Philosophy*, p. 491.

ultimate, known to us as the objective psyche, or field of immediate knowledge. In turn this objective psyche ultimately may be revealed as the x factor researchers in parapsychology are seeking—the medium through which ESP information is "transmitted" and through which other "psi" phenomena occur. The individual who consults the *I Ching* is confronted with this medium of parapsychological phenomena itself; it is a medium that contains certain structures or archetypes which complement the activities of the phenomenological world. It is these structures that are symbolized by the hexagrams.

Thus far we have only briefly touched upon the significance of numerical symbolism, which is peculiar to the archetypal ground of the *I Ching*. That is, the whole of the divinatory process employed in this occult art arises out of certain qualitative relationships between certain key numbers. This peculiarity, as we shall soon see, is shared with other occult systems and appears to be the ultimate symbolic expression of this ground.

Furthermore, both the *I Ching* and astrology appear to be symbolic structures organized around the manifestation of a central energic principle about which these numerical qualities "speak." The *I Ching* tells us that what is being activated is a numerical dimension, or at least a dimension that can express itself only through number. What is peculiar about this operation is that number in every instance is employed qualitatively. Invariably, number represents a quality rather than a quantity when it is presented to us as a statement about the dimension of the objective psyche. The most illustrative instance of this usage of number as quality is to be found in Kabbalism, the focus of our next chapter.

3

The Structure of God

> The ancients, indeed, did not ask why nature submits to laws, but why it is ordered according to genera.
>
> —Henri Bergson

THE KABBALAH is not an occult art in the modern sense of the word. Such arts, as we have seen with astrology and the *I Ching,* have their origin in philosophic ideas no longer deemed viable by the Western rational mind. Kabbalism was and still is the mystical branch of Judaism. This is not to say that it does not contain philosophic speculation of the first order, but because of its religious nature it has been relegated to the dark corners of history's intellectual achievements. So pervasive and electrifying is its thought, however, that early European occultists who did concern themselves with philosophic speculation were immediately drawn to the insights contained within Kabbalistic texts. Much of the excitement prompted by Kabbalism was caused by its speculative inquiries into the nature of the soul, the creation of the universe, and the operations of God. This branch of Kabbalism had its origin in the *Ma'aseh Bereshith* ("story of creation") as given us in the first Book of Genesis.

The second branch of Kabbalism, known as the practical or magical branch, had its origin in the *Ma'aseh*

Merkabah ("story of the divine throne or chariot"), the mystical adoration of the throne-chariot of God as described in the first chapter of Ezekiel. The *Merkabah* mystics were ecstatic visionaries who had little to do with philosophic speculation. Their ends were purely shamanistic in that they sought nothing more than a means to pass through the seven heavenly halls of heaven so that they might come before the throne-chariot. To accomplish this end—an achievement not without its perils, for before each hall stood a guardian demon to be appeased—they created a great number of magical amulets and incantations. This early involvement with what may generally be termed magical devices, but more properly shamanistic techniques, never reflected an attempt to control the powers of heaven or the demonic agencies therein for mundane purposes. The entire procedure was a rite of spiritual passage. Several of these techniques would eventually be employed by those practitioners of speculative Kabbalism as well with the same end in mind.

As in every culture, the secular Jew of the Middle Ages was victim to the common folk-belief in demons, evil spirits, possession, and the efficacy of magical preparations and spells to procure good fortune and ward off evil. It did not take long before the method and nomenclature of *Merkabah* mysticism in particular and Kabbalism in general was adopted by the man in the street. This new accretion was then called Kabbalism by the Jews themselves. No one bothered to notice that the scope and purpose of the magical rites in question no longer had anything to do with the goals of religion. In such a manner did the type of magic peculiar to Euro-

pean culture during the Middle Ages take on the garb
of Kabbalism, which would from that time forward be
mistaken for an "occult" or "magical" art.

The few occultists who concerned themselves with
speculative Kabbalism (and should therefore be called
philosophers in the Oriental sense of the term) also borrowed from Jewish mysticism, oftentimes marrying Kabbalism with Neoplatonic thought. What obviously at-
tracted them to this mysticism was the similarity in
philosophic pattern underlying its metaphysical structure. The adoption of certain key Kabbalistic ideas by
these thinkers therefore demands that we discuss it, for
it not only sheds further light on the workings of the occult arts, but defines the operations of the field of immediate knowledge we discussed in our last chapter.

In so short a space we shall not be able to present the
whole range of Kabbalistic speculation, but will instead
concentrate on four major principles: the En-Sof and
the configurations of the *Sefiroth,* the alphabet and its
symbolism, and the four-world system.

The En-Sof and the Configuration of the Sefiroth

The En-Sof (the 'Limitless" or "Boundless") is thought
of by the Kabbalists as the Divine Principle, or God,
standing above the God of the Bible. By definition the
En-Sof is without definition and is often described by
the Kabbalists as being that which is no-thing, limitless,
without location in either time or space, and without desire or impulse. A considerable amount of speculation
concerning the operation of the En-Sof and the creation
of the universe has been left to us by the Kabbalists,

but in terms of originality and philosophic worth little compares with that left us by Isaac Luria (1533–1572).

In Luria's system we are told that originally the En-Sof occupied the whole of space or eternity prior to his contraction into himself in the form of a single point. By this self-imposed contraction the En-Sof left behind the emptiness that was to become the universe. In this space the activity of Genesis then transpired through the agency of the En-Sof's only willful operation, which constituted no more than the beaming out of a ray of light onto the skein of emptiness. Where this ray struck, there appeared a pinpoint of light. This idea was obviously borrowed from the thirteenth-century classic, the *Zohar*, or *Book of Splendor*. Written by Moses de Leon (Moses ben Shemtob de Leon), the *Zohar* is the only Kabbalistic work to have become a canonical text, practically on the same footing as the Talmud and the Bible. Reference to the emanation of a ray of light from the En-Sof into a pinpoint of light is made in the following passage from De Leon's seminal work:

> At the outset the decision of the King made a tracing in the supernal effulgence, a lamp of scintillation, and there issued within the impenetrable recesses of the mysterious limitless a shapeless nucleus enclosed in a ring, neither white nor black nor red nor green nor of any colour at all. When he took measurements, he fashioned colours to show within, and within the lamp there issued a certain effluence from which colours were imprinted below. The most mysterious Power enshrouded in the limitless clave, as it were, without cleaving its void, remaining wholly unknowable until from the force of the strokes there shone forth a supernal and myste-

rious point. Beyond that point there is no knowable
and therefore it is called *Reshith* (beginning), the
creative utterance which is the starting-point of all.[1]

The appearance of this spark in the void signals the
emanation of the *Sefiroth,* the principles representative
of the En-Sof's totality, some of which are believed to
be within the range of man's consciousness. From the
section of the *Zohar* entitled "The Lesser Holy Assem-
bly" we find a description of the extension of this spark
into the *Sefiroth*:

> The most Ancient One [the En-Sof] is at the same
> time the most Hidden of the hidden. . . . He made
> ten lights spring forth from his midst, lights which
> shine with the form which they have borrowed
> from Him, and which shed everywhere the light of
> a brilliant day. The Ancient One, the most Hidden
> of the hidden, is a high beacon, and we know Him
> only by His lights, which illuminate our eyes so
> abundantly. His Holy Name is no other thing than
> these lights.[2]

The Kabbalists depict the configuration of the *Sefiroth*
by the diagram familiar to all occultists.[3]

In Hebrew the term *Sefiroth* means simply "numbers,"
the theory of which is first found in the famous *Sefer
Yetzirah,* or *Book of Creation,* where we read:

> The Ten ineffable Sephiroth have the appearance of
> the Lightning flash, their origin is unseen and no

[1] *The Zohar,* trans. by Harry Sperling and Maurice Simon (New
York: Rebecca Bennett Publications, 1958), p. 63.
[2] J. Abelson, *Jewish Mysticism* (London: G. Bell & Sons, 1913),
p. 137.
[3] See Figure 12, p. 130.

end is perceived. The Word is in them as they rush
forth and as they return, they speak as from the
whirlwind, and returning fall prostrate in adoration
before the Throne. . . . The ineffable Sephiroth give
forth the Ten numbers. . . . Behold! From the Ten
ineffable Sephiroth do proceed—the One Spirit of
the Gods of the living, Air, Water, Fire; and also
Height, Depth, East, West, North and South.[4]

The following is a brief description of each of the
Sefiroth.

1. Kether ("crown") is also known as the Old or Ancient One, the Primordial Point or Monad, the Ancient
of Ancients, the Smooth Point, the White Head, the
Inscrutable Height, and the Vast Countenance or
Macroprosopus.

It is believed that the entire plan of the creation was
originally contained in this *Sefirah*, which corresponds
with the God of the Old Testament. In Kabbalistic
thought, it is referred to as Knowledge, and in accordance with the idea that it may be only partially known,
is illustrated as the profile of an old man. Out of this
Sefirah emanate Hokhmah and Binah.

2. Hokhmah ("wisdom") is also called the Father of
all Fathers, or *Abba*, and is therefore known as masculine. Whereas in the *Sefirah* Kether we had the plan of
creation, in Hokhmah we have in addition to the plan of
creation the will to create. In speaking of this *Sefirah*,
the Kabbalists often refer us to Psalms 104:24: "O Lord,
how manifold are thy works! In wisdom hast thou made
them all."

---

[4] *Sepher Yetzirah—The Book of Formation*, trans. by Wm. Wynn
Westcott, M.B. (New York: Occult Research Press, n.d.), pp. 16 ff.

In contrast to Kether's role as Knowledge, Hokhmah is the Knower.

3. Binah ("understanding," or "intelligence") is *Imma*, the Supernal Mother, and represents that which is known. The Kabbalists believed that everything contained in Hokhmah *in potentia* was given birth through the agency of this *Sefirah*, which therefore has the attribute of "womb" assigned it.

With the appearance of the second and third *Sefiroth*, the differentiation of the sexes came into being. Kether, Hokhmah, Hesed, and Netsah are labeled masculine; Binah, Gevurah, Hod, and Malkuth, feminine; Tifereth and Yesod are mediators and bisexual. (See Figure 11.)

The *Sefiroth* are seen as emanating in triadic formation. The first triad represents the divine thought of God. The second triadic formation is composed of Hesed, Gevurah, and Tifereth.

4. Hesed ("love," or "mercy") is the product of the union of wisdom and understanding and represents the productive and life-giving power in the universe.

Whereas the first triad represented the dynamics of knowledge, this *Sefirah* introduces the theme for the second triad—will. Hesed represents the expansion of will.

5. Gevurah ("power," or "judgment") expresses the balance of mercy, the idea being that if mercy existed without the quality of judgment or control, it would degenerate into weakness. Mercy balances this *Sefirah* by modifying the power of judgment, which without restraints would become cruelty. While the fourth *Sefirah* possesses an expansive quality (the expansive will), the fifth balances with a contracting force and is called contraction of will.

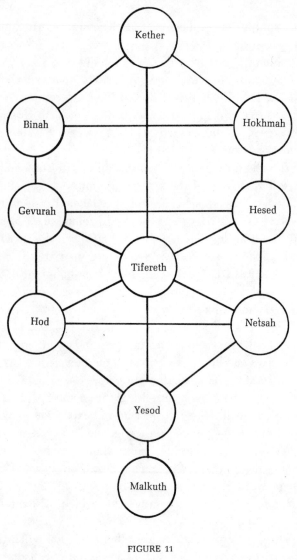

FIGURE 11
THE SEFIROTH

6. Tifereth ("beauty") is also known as the Microprosopus, or the Lesser Countenance. The Microprosopus represents both manifest and unmanifest in contrast to the Macroprosopus, symbolized by the *Sefirah* Kether, which is more commonly known to the Kabbalists as Adam Kadmon, or the Primordial Man of Genesis. The Microprosopus is composed of Tifereth and the six *Sefiroth* Hesed, Gevurah, Tifereth, Netsah, Hod, and Yesod; and symbolizes in pictorial representation a full view of Adam Kadmon's body from the rear.[5]

With the manifestation of the *Sefirah* Tifereth, the second triad of the *Sefiroth* is complete, and stands for God's moral power.

7. Netsah ("victory," or "endurance") is the first of the triad representative of the material universe in the multiplicity of forms.

8. Hod ("majesty," or "glory") is feminine and passive in nature.

9. Yesod ("foundation") represents the male and female genitals and completes the last triadic division of the *Sefiroth*. Symbolically, it stands for God's reproductive or creative powers as manifested in the world through the agency of man.

10. Malkuth ("kingdom") is known as God's feminine counterpart, the Shekinah.

The *Sefiroth* are generally considered to operate outside of and beyond the immediate sphere of the En-Sof. In actuality, through a close examination of Kabbalistic

---

[5] Each of the six *Sefiroth* is thought of as composing a portion of Adam Kadmon: Hesed and Gevurah, the right and left arms; Netsah and Hod, the right and left legs; Tifereth, the trunk; and Yesod, the male and female genitals.

doctrine, we discover that the *Sefiroth* actually represent the inner dynamics of the En-Sof itself. That is, they symbolize the dynamic process of God's mind and of the creative process in particular. The statement by later Kabbalists to the effect that the *Sefiroth* represent the operations of man's mind led to far-reaching conclusions about the location of the En-Sof, a point we shall take up at the end of this chapter.

The Hebrew Alphabet

The emanation of God in the form of divine energy contained in the configuration of the *Sefiroth* also marshaled the creation of a divine language expressive of the structural dynamic inherent in the En-Sof. The three primordial substances of water, fire, and air were synonyms for the three "mother" letters *aleph, mem,* and *shin* which represent the cardinal divisions of the Hebrew alphabet: "The three Mothers in the world are Aleph, Mem and Shin: the heavens were produced from Fire; the earth from the Water; and the Air from the Spirit is as a reconciler between the Fire and the Water." [6]

The letter *aleph* is an aspirate, a letter enunciated with a silent breathing. Hence the assignment of the element air. *Mem* belongs to the class of mutes, which are enunciated by the silent pressing of the lips. Because of all creatures the fish is most symbolic of muteness, and because the first letter of the Hebrew word for fish is *mem,* the letter is associated with the element water. The final "mother," *shin,* belongs to the class of sibilants,

[6] *Sepher Yetzirah,* p. 19.

those letters pronounced with a hissing sound. The Hebrew word for fire is *esh*, hence the association of *shin* with fire.

In addition to these associations with the elements, the mother letters also correspond to the seasons of the year; *shin* (fire) represents the summer season; *mem* (water), the winter; and *aleph* (air), spring and autumn. A further association is the correspondence between these letters and the human body: The head is thought of as being formed by fire (*shin*), the stomach by water (*mem*), and the chest by air (*aleph*).

Besides the three mother letters there are seven double letters, so-called because they represent two sounds, one positive and strong, the other negative and soft; these are also symbolic of opposite qualities—for instance, *beth* represents life and death, and *pe* represents grace and sin. The *Sefer Yetzirah* also tells us that God produced the planets, the days of the week, and the gates of the soul—the two eyes, two ears, two nostrils, and the mouth—with the aid of these seven double letters. The remaining twelve simple letters of the Hebrew alphabet correspond to the senses, emotions, and astrological signs.

If one takes the schema of the seven double letters and assigns them to the compass points they symbolize, adding to this the astrological signs associated with the twelve simple letters, one arrives at a mandala. Whereas the configuration of the *Sefiroth* represents the figure of the divine *anthropos*, Adam Kadmon, this mandala specifically refers us to the physical body, its instincts and temperaments, and the departments of life symbolized by the double letters.

The Hebrew alphabet is in its own right a model of the universe, a system illustrative of the ordering principle lying at the base of the universe to which are also assigned numerical values instrumental in the art of permutation.

Gematria

The first art of Kabbalistic permutation is gematria, in which the letters of a word are converted into their numerical equivalent thereby causing a correspondence be-

THE HEBREW ALPHABET AND ITS SYMBOLIC ASPECTS

	aleph	(A) air	1	spring and autumn	
	beth	(B)	2	life and death	above
	gimel	(G)	3	peace and war	
	daleth	(D)	4	knowledge and ignorance	east
Aries	*he*	(H)	5	foundation of sight	
Taurus	*vau*	(U or V)	6	foundation of hearing	
Gemini	*zain*	(Z)	7	foundation of smelling	
Cancer	*cheth*	(Ch)	8	foundation of speech	
Leo	*teth*	(Th)	9	foundation of taste and digestive organs	
Virgo	*yod*	(I, Y, or J)	10	foundation of sexual love	
	kaph	(K)	20°	wealth and poverty	west
Libra	*lamed*	(L)	30	foundation of activity or work	
	mem	(M) water	40°	winter	
Scorpio	*nun*	(N)	50°	foundation of movement	
Sagittarius	*samekh*	(S)	60	foundation of anger	
Capricorn	*ain*	(O)	70	foundation of mirth	
	pe	(P)	80°	grace and sin	north
Aquarius	*tzaddi*	(Tz)	90°	foundation of imagination	
Pisces	*qoph*	(Q)	100	foundation of sleep	
	resh	(R)	200	fertility and sterility	south
	shin	(Sh) fire	300	summer	
	tau	(T)	400	power and slavery	center

° As final letters, K, M, N, P, and Tz have the numerical values of 500, 600, 700, 800, and 900 respectively.

tween it and any number of other words bearing the same numerical value. By this method one word may represent several ideas beyond its lexicographical meaning.

Notarikon

There are two methods of notarikon, each aiming at abbreviation. The first method involves the forming of one word by the selection of the initial and final letters of another word or words. The second form involves the selection of the initial or final letters of words contained within a sentence. The word *amen* (AMN) comes to us through notarikon from the phrase "the Lord and faithful king" (*Adonai melekh namen*).

Temura

The final form of permutation is the most complicated of all in that there are approximately twenty-five different methods one may employ. The simplest is one in which one-half of the Hebrew alphabet is reversed and placed over the remaining half, which is in the proper order:

k	i	th	ch	z	v	h	d	g	b	a
l	m	n	s	o	p	tz	q	r	sh	t

An example of how this method was employed is to be found in Jeremiah 25:26, where we find the word *sheshak*. Reference is later made (Jeremiah 51:41) to *sheshak* as babel. This is a permutation arrived at by substituting the letters in one name for the letters found either above or below in the ordering shown above.

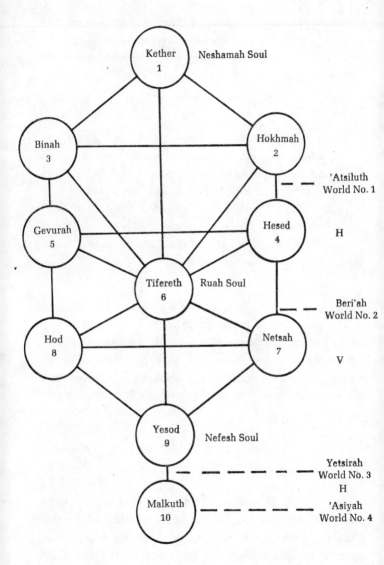

FIGURE 12

sh	sh	k	sh	(e)sh	(a)k
b	b	l	b	(a)b	(e)l

The Four Worlds

The final aspect of the Kabbalistic ideas to be presented here is the concept of the four worlds, which theorizes that the expression of the En-Sof resulted in four levels of reality.

The first world is *'atsiluth,* the world of emanation where God first manifested himself in the form of the archetypal principles defined as *Sefiroth.* The second world, *beri'ah,* is the world of creation or of creative ideas. It is there that the throne-chariot of Ezekiel's vision is to be found along with the highest-ranking angels and the pure spirits of the pious. The third world, *yetsirah,* is the world of formation wherein are contained the seven halls or heavens that lead up to the throne-chariot of God.

The original emanation of the En-Sof diminishes in quality and potency in its descent until finally the impurities formed during its passage into the void of our universe gather to form the world of matter that is ours. This fourth world is called *'asiyah,* or the world of making. It is in this world that the exiled feminine portion of God, the shekinah, resides along with the evil spirits known as the *kelippoth* ("outer shells").

This scheme of the four worlds is one of many and the simplest. Two alternative schemes, however, which figure in tarot divination, the topic of our next chapter, must be discussed before we close this section.

The second system states that each world contains the ten *Sefiroth* in their entirety, each presentation of the configuration of the *Sefiroth,* however, diminishing in quality and potency. The third scheme is a bit more complex but far more imaginative and suggestive than either of the preceding.

In this latter system the *Sefiroth* are distributed over the course of the four worlds. The first world, *'atsiluth,* contains the first triad of the *Sefiroth;* the second world, *beri'ah,* contains the second triad; *yetsirah,* the third world and triad; the fourth world, *'asiyah,* symbolizes our world.

Appended to this scheme of the four worlds is the Kabbalistic doctrine of the triple division of the soul. The *Neshamah,* the highest degree of the soul and its rational element, corresponds to the *Sefirah* Kether located in the first world. The second division of the soul, *Ruah,* the moral element, corresponds to the *Sefirah* Tifereth located in the second world. The third division of the soul, *Nefesh,* which contains the animal life and its desires, corresponds to the *Sefirah* Yesod and the third world. The fourth world is without soul.

The last doctrine appended to the four-world system is that of the tetragrammaton. According to Kabbalistic tradition there are several names by which God may be known, but the most effective and representative of his powers is the tetragrammaton ("the word of four letters," the "square name"), written IHVH. The *Zohar* tells us that God's name became manifest along with the creation of the world. In other words, the *Sefiroth* and the letters of God's name correspond to one another: The point at the top of the letter *yod* (I) symbolizes the *Sefirah* Kether; the trunk of the letter *yod* corresponds to the *Sefirah* Hokhmah. The first *he* (H) is the *Sefirah* Binah; and the *vau* (V) contains the *Sefiroth*

Hesed, Gevurah, Tifereth, Netsah, and Hod. The final
and second *he* (H) comprises the *Sefirah* Malkuth. (See
Figure 12 for the complete scheme of the *Sefiroth*,
the four worlds, the division of the soul, and the
tetragrammaton.)

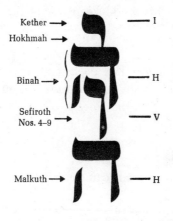

Kether ⟶
Hokhmah ⟶
— I

Binah ⟶
— H

Sefiroth
Nos. 4–9 ⟶
— V

Malkuth ⟶
— H

FIGURE 13

It should also be noticed that Figure 13, the representation of the letters of the tetragrammaton, is a caricature
of the human body. The implication here is that the
whole of the symbolic attributes discussed in this chapter actually constitute the "body" of man; that is, they
are principles contained *in* man, processes of a suprarational dimension intimately united with man's somatic
system.

Man, therefore, along with the *anthropos*, contains
within him the four-fold structure of the worlds that in
certain respects might correspond to four degrees of
consciousness, the fourth world corresponding to normal
waking consciousness.

The whole drift of my education goes to persuade me that the world of our present consciousness is only one out of many worlds of consciousness that exist, and that those other worlds must contain experiences which have a meaning for our life also; and that although in the main their experiences and those of this world keep discrete, yet the two become continuous at certain points, and higher energies filter in.[7]

If William James had been familiar with the Kabbalistic doctrine of the four worlds, he might very well have agreed that the energies contained within the upper three worlds are the "higher energies" he referred to. In recent experiments involving LSD and different levels of consciousness, it was noted that subjects often experienced the presence of electrical phenomena:

At times electrical energy may seem to flow in a pattern corresponding to the peripheral nervous system; at times it may seem to ascend the spinal column from its base, bursting into the brain—an experience also described by adepts of Yoga as the kundalini force.[8]

This also suggests that a psychic energy of some kind might be operative in the scheme of the four worlds. We have already discussed the idea that the occult arts are the products of a central energic principle whose ground ultimately expresses itself through the agency of

[7] William James, *The Varieties of Religious Experience* (New York: Longmans, Green, 1910), p. 519.
[8] Walter N. Pahnke and William A. Richards, "Implications of LSD and Experimental Mysticism," in Charles T. Tart, ed., *Altered States of Consciousness: A Book of Readings* (New York: John Wiley, 1969), p. 412.

number. As we have just seen in our discussion of the *Sefroth,* the manifestation of number is an expression of a central and transcendant principle known as the En-Sof, an inexhaustible plenum of energy.

This central principle, which we identified as the field of absolute knowledge in agreement with Jung, ultimately expresses itself in symbolic modes of which the occult arts is but one. Another such mode, which may already have become apparent to the reader, is language, or more specifically, the alphabet. The following discussion will seek to develop the relationship between energy, number, and the alphabet as expressed in Kabbalism and their relevance in light of certain scientific and philosophic thought in the twentieth century.

The Cosmos as Energy

To understand such principles as the Tao and the En-Sof as exemplary of a quantum of nonspecific energy, it is first necessary to realize that the first products of their expression, their initial manifestation in mundane reality as imagined by mystics and metaphysicians, is in the form of polarities: male-female, yin-yang, dark-light, above-below, good-bad, and the like. Inherent in the representation of these polarities is the idea of tension, each polarity expressive of either a diminution or an amplification of a quality or condition that in the last analysis may be recognized as a state of energy. Invariably we are informed that these polarities initially existed in a state of union within the body of a prime principle—in this case the En-Sof.

In Lurianic Kabbalism the *Sefiroth* appeared first as empty vessels, and not until the outpouring of light from the En-Sof into these vessels did they become active principles. In other words, this original energic principle is without specific form and must create forms in which it may be contained. Implicit in this metaphysical system is the idea that all things, especially living organisms, contain vestiges of this energic source. The significance of a concept of energy that imbues not only categorical and divine principles with meaning, the *Sefiroth* in this instance, but also the entire universe and man himself is only now becoming plausible to the scientific community.

A recent work describing parapsychological research in the Soviet Union and other iron-curtain countries revealed the existence of a new method capable of photographing the energy fields surrounding living matter.[9] The method is known as Kirlian photography, and to all appearances it records the energy field that many occultists in the past claimed existed around all living matter —the aura. Photographs of leaves, human hands, and other objects revealed a cosmic array of colors, flares, and sparks emanating from their surfaces. Taking a fresh leaf, the researchers watched the pulsating flares and wondered if they actually referred to a life-force. Their experiments with withered and dead leaves answered in the affirmative. A withered leaf's pulsations were less noticeable, the colors less pronounced. A dead leaf showed neither color nor pulsations. Photographing the finger of a normal, even-tempered, rested man, the researchers discovered an even distribution of "energy

[9] Sheila Ostrander and Lynn Schroeder, *Psychic Discoveries Behind the Iron Curtain* (New York: Bantam Books, 1971).

flares" streaming from his finger. The same man, photographed when tired, revealed enormous charges of energy flares streaming from his finger, a visual confirmation of a "loss of energy."

Of further significance for our purposes was the meeting of the authors, Sheila Ostrander and Lynn Schroeder, with a young student of Kirlian photography. He showed them two photographs of the same leaf, the patterns of which were identical with but one exception: The sparkling lines on the pattern in the upper-right-hand portion of the leaf in one photograph were not as finely defined as they were in the other. The young scientist explained that the photograph in question was that of the leaf with one-third of itself missing. In other words, the photograph revealed a phantom energy field. The cutaway portion of the leaf left behind a pattern representative of its original outline.

The "phantom-limb" phenomenon reported by amputees claiming that they experienced sensation in areas once occupied by their missing limbs may be further indication of the existence of phantom energy fields. Many such claims, generally attributed to either imagination or brain damage, may actually refer to the awareness of such fields by the afflicted person. At the other end of the spectrum we have the experiences of schizophrenics who experience loss of body boundary and are unable to distinguish locations where sensations are originating, whether inside or outside of their bodies. More extreme cases report the displacement of limbs into far corners of a room: "In bed I kept my eyes shut so I didn't see people but I heard them. Touch was all important.

Sometimes my body seemed apart, a leg or an arm across the room.[10]

These experiences and others reminiscent of a "going-to-pieces" feeling may actually be descriptive of a breakdown of this energy pattern underlying our physical bodies. That the astrological archetype, the configuration of the *Sefiroth,* and the diagram of earlier and later heaven of the *I Ching* all assign their individual symbolic values to portions of the human body may be of considerable relevance. These microcosmic delineations may be nothing more than a symbolic depiction of the "natural" energy-field pattern revealed by Kirlian photography. Furthermore there are indications in the research of Clyde Backster that this energy-field phenomenon discovered by Kirlian is not just a matter of electrostatic patterns, a lifeless energy source, but actually yet another field of consciousness.

Formerly employed by the Central Intelligence Agency and the U.S. Counter Intelligence Corps as a polygraph expert, Backster has discovered that plants not only operate within a large communication field but are also capable of reading minds, experiencing emotions, and retaining memory. While experiments providing the validity of such statements are not the immediate subject of this book, we will consider one of Backster's experiments because it reveals material important to our line of investigation.

One day Backster hooked his polygraph machine up to a nonincubated fresh egg and received recorded cycles of approximately 170 beats per minute. This is the

[10] James S. Gordon, "Who Is Mad? Who Is Sane?," in Hendrik M. Ruitenbeek, ed., *Going Crazy* (New York: Bantam Books, 1972), p. 93.

cycle that would normally be found in a chick embryo three to four days old in incubation. When Backster opened the egg to assure himself that what he was testing was a nonincubated egg, he could nowhere discover a physical circulatory system. As one interviewer put it, "Is there, Backster wonders, an 'energy field blueprint' providing a rhythm and pattern about which matter coalesces to form organic structure? . . . Does the 'idea' of an organism precede its material development?" [11]

In addition to this, Backster discovered that this energy field, which serves as a communication link between plants and other animate things,

> is not within the different known frequencies AM, FM, or any form of signal which we can shield by ordinary means . . . and distance doesn't seem to impose any limitation. I've tried shielding the plants with a Faraday screen cage (which prevents electrical penetration), even lead-lined containers. It seems that the signal may not fall within any known portion of our electrodynamic spectrum. [12]

Yet, through some as yet unknown process the signal transforms itself into a recordable electric current. The reader may recall our previous references to a field in which "energy" of some sort may be transmitted in ESP experiments. Backster appears to have stumbled onto this energy itself. As in the experiments of Rhine and Schmeidler, his work also demonstrated that distance has no effect on the signal, nor do containers, rooms, buildings, etc. Again we are in the presence of this mys-

[11] John M. White, "Plants, Polygraphs, and Paraphysics," *Psychic*, Vol. III (December, 1972), p. 15.
[12] *Ibid.*, p. 14.

terious energy about which nothing concrete is known.

A Kabbalist might interpret the above material by stating that the nonspecific forms of energy, the communication field within which plants communicate with one another and other living beings, along with, perhaps, the aura revealed by Kirlian photography, are examples of the effusion of the En-Sof as an energic principle in the world. Similarly, the underlying patterns, as in the Backster experiment with the egg, point to the imprinting of the configuration of the *Sefiroth* on matter as a potential life-structure. Our argument may be weak up to this point, but in the following discussion of number and language the picture loses some of its haziness.

The Alphabet as Algebra

If nothing else the *Sefiroth* represent the numerical categories of a transcendant principle of unity. It is the principle that the astrologers pointed to when they devised the archetype, the Chinese when they outlined the nature of the Tao, and the Kabbalists when they described the operations of the En-Sof and the *Sefiroth*.

It must be appreciated that number was initially experienced as qualities of "oneness, twoness, threeness," all of which was initially bound up with symbolic connotations. To the Pythagoreans, for example, the number 5 was symbolic of marriage because it is the product of the first masculine number, 3, and the first feminine, 2. Therefore, it was the "fiveness" of a group of objects that was important rather than the abstract arithmetical matrix of the group. Behind all of this was the idea of an original unity symbolized by 1. This is what some philosophers refer us to when they discuss the existence of another "condition" of number.

One good example of this condition may be found in the tenth book of the *Confessions of St. Augustine,* where we find Augustine recording his experiences in what he calls the "large and boundless chamber" of memory, the bottom of which "has never been sounded":

> I have perceived also the numbers of the things with which we number all the senses of my body: *but those numbers wherewith we number are different.* Nor are they the images of these, and therefore they indeed are. Let him who seeth them not, deride me for saying these things, and I will pity him, while he derides me.[13]

Clearly, along with the implication that numbers are expressive of God Himself, reference is made here to the existence of a set of numbers that exists above and beyond number as we know it. This too is the idea behind Nicholas of Cusa's statement that "number is the first model of things in the mind of the Creator." What we have in the configuration of the *Sefiroth* is the "first model of things" as understood by the Kabbalists. One mathematician understood the significance of this idea when, in discussing the nature of mathematics, he wrote:

> Mathematics is placed in a field of knowledge between two complementary poles: one the world of reality called exterior, the other, interior. These two

---

[13] St. Augustine, in Charles W. Eliot, ed., *The Harvard Classics,* Vol. VII: *The Confessions of St. Augustine* (New York: P. F. Collier & Sons, 1909–1910), p. 170; italics mine.

worlds are beyond consciousness. They are not graspable as such, but their imprints appear in the field of consciousness. Mathematics shows this double imprint.[14]

Pythagoras was the first to discern this inherent duality in the phenomenon of number by recognizing that while exempt from the limitations of time and space, number nontheless played a significant role in these two arenas. Whereas there is always the possibility of natural phenomena going awry, fish walking on earth and birds swimming beneath the water, for instance, nothing can ever change the fact that two plus two equals four. On the other hand, because Pythagoras believed the ultimate stuff of the universe was number, number influenced the creation and dynamics of the world. We find the further development of this idea in Plotinus:

> Besides Intelligence, and anterior thereto, exists Essence. It contains Number, with which it begets (beings): for it begets them by moving according to number, determining upon the numbers before giving hypostatic existence to the (beings), just as the unity (of essence) precedes its (existence), and interrelates it with the First (or, absolute Unity).[15]

Many of us might recall with what difficulty we encountered the phenomenon of number as abstraction when as children we were asked to appreciate that five apples and five cars had a relationship that had nothing to do with either the quality or the function of the ob-

[14] Quoted in Marie-Louise von Franz, "The Dream of Descartes," in James Hillman, ed., *Timeless Documents of the Soul* (Evanston, Ill.: Northwestern University Press, 1968), p. 71.

[15] *The Works of Plotinus,* trans. and ed. by Kenneth Sylvan Guthrie, Vol. III (London: George Bell & Sons, 1918), p. 670.

jects in question. Modern man takes this ability for abstract thinking for granted, but to ancient man number had an individual personality with far-reaching implications. Therefore, such early philosophic statements discussing the duality of number signals the advent of an unprecedented extension of scientific awareness and consciousness. We might then think of the earlier qualitative concerns with number as unconscious expressions of an inherent order existing either in the universe itself or 'in man, where it is expressive of hidden cerebral or neural structures.

With this concern with numbers as qualitative principles is a related involvement with letters of the alphabet, divine names, and magical words. As the noted authority on Jewish mysticism, Gershom Scholem, has observed:

> The secret world of the godhead is a world of language, a world of divine names that unfold in accordance with a law of their own. . . . Letters and names are not only conventional means of communication. They are more. Each one of them represents a concentration of energy and expresses a wealth of meaning which cannot be translated, or not fully at least, into human language.[16]

In Kabbalism, as in other systems that employ numbers and letters as mystical instruments, there appears to be a confusion over whether it was numbers or letters that were initially employed in the creation of the world. Whereas in one instance, in the *Sefer Yetzirah*, we are told that number in the form of the *Sefiroth* de-

---

[16] Gershom G. Scholem, *On the Kabbalah* (New York: Schocken Books, 1965), p. 35.

fined the arena of space and time, a few chapters later we find: "Twenty-two letters: He drew them, hewed them, combined them, weighed them, interchanged them, and through this produced the whole of creation and everything that is destined to come into being." [17]

And nowhere do we find Kabbalists complaining of this paradox. Similarly, in the *Zohar* there are statements to the effect that the universe was created through the agency of number in one passage, and in another:

> Aleph, Aleph, although I will begin the creation of the world with the beth, thou wilt remain the first of the letters. My unity shall not be expressed except through thee, on thee shall be based all *calculations and operations* of the world, and unity shall not be expressed save by the letter Aleph. [18]

From these seemingly accepted contradictory points of view, we can only assume that the men who wrote of these things understood the two systems of number and alphabet to be of one and the same fabric. Letters along with numbers may be seen as emblematic of a supreme power or ordering principle that initially impresses its existence upon reality through their agency. One might, then, discover in language not only a structural universality but an order essentially mathematical in proportion. Such an idea can then lead us to consider the thought of Noam Chomsky, professor of linguistics at the Massachusetts Institute of Technology.

The prevailing explanation of the process of language

---

[17] Quoted in J. Abelson, *Jewish Mysticism* (London: George Bell & Sons, 1913), p. 101.
[18] *The Zohar*, p. 13; italics mine.

learning for the past three centuries has been the empirical premise that language is learned through experience and that the experience of language is simply a matter of habit. Chomsky, on the other hand, has suggested that there are "formal linguistic universals," or a "principle of universal grammar." It is his belief that a child is born with these universal principles of grammar already present in his brain: "It does seem quite reasonable to propose . . . that the unknown structures of the brain that provide knowledge of language on the basis of the limited data available to us 'possess within themselves' the idea of structure-dependent operations." [19]

These "structure-dependent operations" have been classified by Chomsky by the term "deep structures," which "apparently are deep-seated and rather abstract principles of a very general nature that determine the form and interpretation of sentences." [20] He also says: "Knowledge of language results from the interplay of initially given structures of mind, maturational processes, and interaction with the environment." [21]

The inevitable conclusion of this line of reasoning is that the rules of transformational grammar, the title given to Chomsky's theories, can be expressed in mathematical notation simply because the domain they explain is expressive of a mathematical symmetry or structure.

> The study of formal properties and generative capacity of various types of grammar exists as a branch of mathematics or logic, independently of its

[19] Noam Chomsky, *Problems of Knowledge and Freedom: The Russell Lectures* (New York: Vintage Books, 1972), p. 29.
[20] *Ibid.*, p. 43.
[21] *Ibid.*, p. 23.

relevance for the description of natural languages
The revolutionary step that Chomsky has taken, has
been to draw upon this branch of mathematics . . .
and to apply it to natural languages . . . rather
than to the artificial languages constructed by logi-
cians and computer scientists.[22]

Most mathematicians would agree with Alfred North
Whitehead's statement: "Mathematics is essentially a
study of types of order." The mathematical formulas of
transformational grammar . could therefore not be applied if an existing structure, mathematically propor-
tioned, did not already exist upon which it could be
imposed.

We are obligated at this point to mention that
Chomsky has denied the existence of any significance
between his theory and the occult attitude toward the
alphabet and language, *vide:*

the careful study of language shows that these operations apply to abstract forms underlying sentences,
to structures that may be quite remote from the actual physical events that constitute spoken or
written language. . . . These structures and the operations that apply to them are postulated as mental
entities in our effort to understand what one has
learned, when he has come to know a language,
and to explain how sentences are formed and understood. I would like to emphasize that there is
nothing strange or occult in this move.[23]

It is nonetheless curious that the trail that led Chomsky to his discoveries began during his undergraduate

[22] John Lyons, *Noam Chomsky* (New York: The Viking Press,
1970), p. 69.
[23] *Ibid.*, p. 32.

years with his sudden involvement with Hebrew, an event that has been described as the turning point in this thought.[24]

All of this suggests that the Kabbalistic concern with number and the letters of the alphabet is essentially an intimation of what Chomsky has named the "deep structures" of language, and that underlying it we may expect to find the energic source in which the ordering principle resides.

The En-Sof of Kabbalism might then be seen as symbolic of an ordering principle operating in the human psyche, if not in the universe itself, whose simple expression may be the nonspecific communications field discovered by Backster. At the same time, the orderly and specific constructs, such as those which appear at the base of the human psyche and the biosphere, may be symbolized by the configuration of the *Sefiroth*. This Kabbalistic diagram may be paradigmatic of a universal principle of order underlying both the cosmos and man. That the revelation of such structures should have first appeared in symbolic mode, in occult, philosophic, religious, and mythological systems, should not blind us to the possibility that they point to truths that, as ambiguous as they may appear at first sight, nonetheless tell us of hidden and viable realities.

The complex relationships to be found between man and the cosmos should make one wary of too hastily adopting a skeptical view. If anything it should suggest that we are only just now beginning to realize the intimacies that exist between man and the universe.

[24] See Daniel Yergin, "The Chomskyan Revolution," *The New York Times Magazine*, December 3, 1972, p. 114.

4

A Metaphysical Melting Pot

He has set each star in its proper zone as a
driver in a chariot . . . he has made
them all dependent on himself, holding that
thus would their march be orderly and
harmonious.

—Philo

WITH THE EXCEPTION of the tarot, all of the occult arts we have discussed so far grew into unified and self-contained systems based on metaphysical ideas that are now practically inseparable from the systems in which they are found. The tarot is more of a pseudoconstruct, a method given substance by the coalescence of metaphysical ideas and elements foreign to each other. Of all the occult arts, it is the youngest. This might explain why the interpretation of its symbols differs from occultist to occultist. It appears that it is just because it does contain the least amount of innate internal structure that it attracts a wide range of interpretative systems to it. Wherever there is a hole in a metaphysical fabric you are sure to find a hundred metaphysicians attempting to fill it. While in comparison the older and more substantial occult arts leave little room for personal interpretation, the tarot is open, beckoning all who pass to contribute. It is for this reason that little may be said of the tarot that has not already been said about those systems it now embodies.

The standard tarot pack contains seventy-eight cards

consisting of two distinct sections called the major trumps and the minor trumps. The major trumps are numbered consecutively from 1 to 22, the zero card thought by some occultists to demand different placements within the series. In addition to this numerical sequence, each card has a title and symbolic picture. The minor trumps, with the exception of an additional card appended to each suit, comprise the standard playing-card deck of fifty-two. The four extra cards, called knaves by some, immediately follow the "jack" of the standard pack. The suits of the tarot differ from our standard suits and have their origin in the Italian tarots of the fourteenth century; cups (*coppe*), swords (*spade*), coins or pentacles (*denare*), and batons or wands (*batone*). The suits of our standard playing cards receive their titles from the French decks of about the same period: spades (*piques*), hearts (*coeurs*), diamonds (*carreaux*), and clubs (*trefles*).

There has been much controversy over the origin of playing cards in general and the tarot in particular, none of which has as yet supplied us with any definite answers. As for the mystical tarot that we have today, it is a matter of conviction among occultists that it reached Europe with the appearance of the Gypsies coming out of India. The fact that the Gypsies did not make an appearance in Europe until the first quarter of the fifteenth century and that tarot cards similar in construction to those we still employ were in use as early as 1379 in Italy has done nothing to dispel the myth.

The major problem in any discussion of the tarot's symbolism lies in the fact that when the system first appeared as an occult device, no interpretative literature came with it. What literature we have today on the subject was created out of hand over the past three centuries. When we seek the source of the major trumps figures, we arrive at a dead end. What little discussion there has been as to the possible meaning and derivation of the figures has mainly centered around the idea that they depict the secret doctrine of a religious tradition. All of which leaves us with the possibility that the roots of the tarot may be lost forever and that if we are to experience any sense of continuity we must turn to its appearance as an occult device.

The Tarot Mystified

It was with the publication by the French philologist Antoine Court de Gebelin (1728–1784) of the eighth volume of his uncompleted *Le Monde primitif, analysé et comparé avec le monde moderne,* that the attention of the Western world was turned toward both Egypt and the tarot. A patient and staunch supporter of Friedrich Anton Mesmer, Gebelin single-handedly gave birth to the theory that the collection of philosophic treatises known to the world as the *Corpus Hermetica* had been created by the mythical Thoth-Hermes along with magic, writing, and language. In addition to this, Gebelin enticed his readers with the following: "If one were to know that in our days there existed a work of Ancient Egypt, one of their books that escaped malicious destruction . . . a book about their most pure and interesting doctrines, everybody would be eager no doubt to know such an extraordinary and precious work." [1]

[1] Antoine Court de Gebelin, quoted in Kurt Seligmann, *The History of Magic* (New York: Pantheon Books, 1948), p. 411.

He then immediately proceeded to explain that the
tarot cards so familiar to Western Europe at that time
constituted the very book he so cryptically spoke of,
and that the term tarot was made up of *Tar*
("way") and *Ro* or *Rog* ("royal," or "kingly"). The illu-
sory scholarship of Gebelin in this and other matters
having to do with Egypt was to be partially overturned
eleven years later with the discovery of the Rosetta
stone in 1799.

Sometime between 1783 and 1787 a French barber
and wigmaker by the name of Alliette, but better known
by the pseudonym he created by reversing the letters of
his name, Etteilla, fell under the influence of Gebelin's
theories. It must be understood that up to the time of
Gebelin's work many different sets of tarot had been
available to the public for gaming purposes and simple
divination. Little concern with design and meaning by
either the general public or the tarot-makers existed.
The sketches of the twenty-two major trumps and four
aces of the tarot given us by Gebelin in his eighth volume appear to have been taken from an existing set,
more than likely the set we now know as the tarot of
Marseilles. Actually the tarot was quite a common thing,
looked upon in much the same manner we today look
upon our playing cards. Gebelin's book changed all of
that. The effect it had would be analogous to that which
would be prompted by the publication of a work in the
twentieth century "proving" that Moses received the
Ten Commandments through the agency of a hula hoop.
It was at this point that the pompous and industrious
Alliette stepped in.

Alliette set out to "correct" not only Gebelin's
sketches, which if nothing else had the authority of tra-

ditional symbolism to recommend them, but also tradition itself by claiming that the secret of the tarot had been lost through mismanagement of the figures. He then quite glibly changed some of the significations, altered a greater portion of the traditional sequence, added his own symbolism, changed the titles of the trumps, and included astrological significations. Immediately upon publication of his Grand Etteilla tarot deck, copies of which may still be purchased, he became one of the leading and most successful soothsayers of Paris.

In such a manner does the concern with the tarot as a *mystical* doctrine begin. From that time on, the tarot was no longer considered just a fortune-telling device. This long line of mystification appears to coalesce around the formation in 1886 of the Order of the Golden Dawn. Through the efforts of the order's members many of the metaphysical arguments having to do with the correct placement of figures within the series, the assignment of Kabbalistic and astrological significations, methods of interpretation, etc., at least took on some semblance of form. Yet to this day you will find disagreement within the ranks of occultists who follow even this system.

In 1854 the celebrated occultist Eliphas Levi (Alphonse Louis Constant) published his monumental *Dogme et rituel de la haute magie* (*Transcendental Magic, Its Doctrine and Ritual*) to supply the "philosophic" foundations of all modern occultism. Much of this philosophy came directly out of his head, only a minor portion of it being gleaned from classical studies. This work was followed in 1856 by his *Rituel* (published in English as *The Ritual of Transcendental Magic*), by which time Alliette's system had fallen into disfavor. But one aspect that Alliette had investigated was again picked up by Levi to be entered into the doctrinal history of the occult: the relationship of Kabbalism with the tarot. Many present-day occultists wrongly ascribe the initial assigning of the Hebrew alphabet to the tarot as the effort of Kabbalist Oswald Wirth. In point of fact the ascription of Hebrew letters, in addition to and not in place of the tarot card numerals, appears on the early tarot cards.

The appearance of Levi's work is a significant moment in occult history. It signaled not only the coming of a metaphysic within which the tarot could gain a specific and "meaningful" structure with historical continuity, but the creation of a catch-all system for the other occult arts as well. Until the appearance of Levi's book each occult art stood on its own foundations, seemingly without a common metaphysical root. True, early in the sixteenth century Henry Cornelius Agrippa von Nettesheim had attempted to give a common ground to these arts with the publication of his *Three Books on Occult Philosophy*, but for some reason his system does not satisfy the modern occultist:

> You are reading Agrippa, and confess to a certain disappointment: did it happen that you took him for a master? He was only a bold vulgariser, and fortunately very superficial in his studies. . . . His work, however, is the first which did something to spread knowledge of the higher sciences. Too shallow for a Magus, he was pleased to pass as a magi-

cian and a sorcerer . . . his books are useful reading
when one knows more and better than he did.[2]

If we consider for a moment the fact that up to the
time of the appearance of the three commentators mentioned above, the tarot was nothing more than a folk device for fortune-telling, without any type of formulated
metaphysic supporting it (in much the same condition
as the *I Ching* before the advent of the Confucians and
Taoists), then the importance of these commentators to
the history of the occult becomes apparent. This is not
to imply that these gentlemen, Levi in particular, have
in any way altered the course of history as did Confu-
cious and Lao-tzu, but rather that the ease with which
they began the tradition that now engages practically
the whole of our media in one way or another is symptomatic of some inherent psychic need that is only now
becoming recognizable. Levi's Kabbalistic and astrological attributions, although not produced by him in card
form, were employed by Oswald Wirth in the production of his tarot cards, now no longer extant but preserved for us by Papus (Dr. Gerard Encausse) in his
The Tarot of the Bohemians, published in 1889.[3]

The next tarot system to appear was given us by A.
E. Waite in the now popular Rider pack, named after
the publishers Rider & Son, who in 1910 published
Waite's *A Pictorial Key to the Tarot,* in which the designs created by Waite first appeared. According to
modern occultists, Waite secretly employed the attribu-

[2] Eliphas Levi, *Transcendental Magic, Its Doctrine and Ritual,*
trans. by Arthur Edward Waite (London: William Rider & Son,
1923), p. 11.
[3] Papus, *The Tarot of the Bohemians,* trans. by A. P. Morton
(New York: Arcanum Books, 1962).

tions given the tarot by the Order of the Golden Dawn. With the advent of the twentieth century, a great flourish of new tarot designs and theories appeared, one of the most peculiar design series being that of Aleister Crowley, published in *The Book of Thoth* (1944). And here the trail ends in a flurry of confusion.

But this history tells us nothing of the tarot prior to the appearance of Court de Gebelin. If we are to postulate the existence of a principle of order that expresses itself as it appears to have done in astrology, the *I Ching*, and Kabbalism, then we should also expect to find in the tarot an indication of a philosophical structure suggestive of this principle. And there does appear to be some indication that an early attempt to incorporate philosophic ideas of the type generally associated with the symbol of the *anthropos* was made with the tarot.

The Fragments of History

If, at the outset, we accede to the premise that at least four of the major trumps contain symbolism borrowed from Greek philosophy, Jewish mysticism and religion, and an allusion to an ancient Persian fire cult—all of which shall be discussed below—then the question that we must pursue is, What group of immigrants to Europe would have had available the broad cultural experience demanded for the creation of the tarot's symbols? There is one bit of information with which we may begin this inquiry.

In Italy, during the latter part of the fourteenth century when the first tarot pack appeared in Europe, the term for play with cards was *naib*. Similarly, in Spain the term was *naipes*. Obviously the two words had a common source, and that source appears to be the Hebrew term for sorcery, *naibi*.[4]

One country the Jews settled in after leaving the Middle East was Spain, where they lived in relative comfort and religious freedom until their explulsion in 1492. It was there that Kabbalism flourished soon after its earlier introduction into Italy in 917 by the Babylonian scholar Aaron ben Samuel. The swan song of the Spanish Jews began in Castile during the year 1371 when the tolerance of the Jews by the Christian community lost its last foothold. In that year the restrictive legislation forcing Jews to wear identifying badges that had taken effect throughout various parts of Spain caught up with the last stronghold of the Spanish Jews. Many began to leave Spain at this time for safer havens, one of which was Italy where for several centuries a number of small Jewish communities had thrived. It is very likely that Kabbalists numbered among those Jews fleeing the country where the famous *Zohar* had been penned by the Kabbalist Moses de Leon.

It was not the first time that Jews were importers of ideas, for centuries earlier they had carried to the Continent the wealth of Alexandrian speculation on such diverse topics as philosophy, mathematics, science, mysticism, and religion. Alexandria was the home of Macedonians, Egyptians, Persians, Antalians, Arabs, Syrians, and Jews. Of its five sections two were populated by Jews. The intellectual flow of ideas in Alexandria at its peak has never since been equaled, nor has any

[4] See Catherine Perry Hargrave, *A History of Playing Cards* (New York: Dover Publications, 1966), p. 224.

world center in ancient history contributed more to the
shaping of Western thought. Because it appears that the
symbolism of the tarot at certain points would have demanded the broad amalgamation of philosophic ideas
that existed in the climate of Alexandria, and because it
was the exodus of the Jews alone that would correspond
to the travel pattern of the ideas necessary for the creation of the tarot (from Alexandria to Spain and to Italy),
the supposition that it was they who might in large part
have contributed to the symbols of the tarot is not a
difficult one to make or to accept.

It is hard to determine exactly when the four trumps
of the tarot became identified with the theory of the
four elements suggested by Aristotle—wands corresponding to fire, cups to water, swords to air, and pentacles to earth—but we do know that by 1509 the
three-element theory of the Kabbalah was supplanted by
the four-element theory in an explication of the *Sefiroth*
by Cornelius Agrippa. The importance of this to our inquiry follows from the identification of the four elements with the Kabbalistic tetragrammaton: I (fire), H
(water), C (air), and H (earth). With this in mind,
two major trump cards of the tarot take on special
significance.

Major trump card 1, the magician, is sometimes given
the title *le bateleur* (the "bearer of the baton or wand,"
or the "juggler"). In his hand he holds a wand (fire),
which has been identified as the paraphernalia of a magician. The objects on the table before him—coins, cups,
and swords—have been interpreted as symbolizing the
three elements air, earth, and water in a state of disar-
ray or chaos. The implication of this symbolism is that

the magician is about to "juggle" the elements, arrange or rearrange them through the influence that he is thought to have over the powers of nature.

The last major trump card, number 21, the world or the universe, depicts the figure of a nude female in the center of an ellipse. In each corner of this card are found one of the following figures: an eagle, a lion, a bull, and the figure of a man or angel. In short, the card is in large part a depiction of the vision given us in Ezekiel 1:10: "As for the likeness of their faces, they four had the face of a man, and the face of a lion, on the right side: and they four had the face of an ox on the left side; they four also had the face of an eagle."

Early in the beginnings of the Christian religion many writers understood this vision to be a depiction of the elements under the guidance of God:

> That is why the prophet [Ezekiel], wanting to show God's presidency and governance of the universe . . . expounds the guidance . . . and intelligent management of the four-faced cherubim as directed by the Logos. . . . Man, being a heavenly plant, corresponds exactly to air; because of his speed, the lion symbolizes fire; the ox symbolizes earth, and the eagle water, because birds are born from water. God, then, . . . holding air and earth, water and fire in his hand and ruling them by his will, like a four-horsed vehicle, in an unutterable way controls . . . the universe and keeps it in being.[5]

Clearly, whoever chose Ezekiel's vision as a depiction of the world for this trump card was not only familiar with the traditional Greek view that the world was com-

[5] Methodius of Olympus, quoted in Jean Danielou, S.J., *Primitive Christian Symbols* (London: Compass Books, 1964), p. 77.

posed of the four elements, but that the vision of the four animals was a metaphor for this idea. This was neither an accidental choice nor an "occult" statement, but was instead a philosophic interpretation of a religious idea. Interpreted as follows, the idea is that the elements are in a state of chaos in the beginning, but through the manipulation by one capable of controlling nature put in order at the end. This view, as we have just seen, might easily have been the construct of Christians who were themselves aware of the correspondences between the vision of Ezekiel and the elements. In addition the figure of the soul in the midst of the four elements on card 21 is a Platonic thought adopted by the church early on. The reason for our still favoring a strong Jewish influence rests in the origins of the term *magus*, which was a word borrowed by the Greeks from the Persians, in Hellenistic times having the following definition: "A *Magus, Magian,* one of a Median tribe . . . 2. *one of the wise men in Persia* who interpreted dreams . . . 3. *any enchanter or wizard,* and in a bad sense, *a juggler,* imposter." [6]

The Median tribe was that part of the Iranian nation in control of Babylonia during the reign of Nebuchadnezzar (d. 562 B.C.), who enslaved the Jews within his city's walls. After their liberation by the Persian king Cyrus in the middle of the sixth century B.C., there arose

[6] Liddell and Scott, *Intermediate Greek-English Lexicon* (New York: Oxford University Press, 1964), p. 483; italics mine. The Jews were allowed freely to continue the expression of their traditions following the destruction of the Achaemenid empire and the capture of Babylonia by Alexander in 331 B.C. Nevertheless, the terms "magus" and "juggler" came to take on a derisive meaning in Greek, as in the third definition.

a tradition among the Jews that some of their rabbis had been jugglers, as can be seen in the following excerpt from the Babylonian Talmud (*Sotah* 22a): "Levi used to juggle in the presence of Rabbi with eight knives, Samuel before King Shapur with eight glasses of wine, and Abaye before Rabbah with eight eggs, or, as some say, with four eggs." Whether our interpretation of the elements found on these two cards is correct or not, it would nonetheless be difficult to deny that the creator of the cards at the very least knew the significance of calling a magician a juggler, or that card 21 portrayed Ezekiel's vision.

In yet another pair of cards, there appear elements that might also be coincidental, but more than likely reveal origins of the tarot. The chariot pictured on trump card 7 is the Greek type, open at the back and drawn by two horses with room only for a standing charioteer. There is every likelihood that the Greeks and Romans brought these along with them from the East, but if they did and if they were ever used on European soil, it is unlikely that such chariots bore the pillars and canopy depicted on the card.

There is an interesting passage to be found in Plato's *Phaedrus* where we find a discussion centering on the nature of relationships between lovers, leading to the idea that the problem in such relationships has to do with the nature of the soul:

> Though her true form be ever a theme of large and more than mortal discourse, let me speak briefly, and in a figure. And let the figure be composite—a pair of winged horses and a charioteer . . . and one of the horses was good and the other bad . . . the right-hand horse is a lover of honour and modesty

and temperance, and the follower of true glory . . .
the other . . . the mate of insolence and pride,
shag-eared, and deaf, hardly yielding to whip and
spur.[7]

The horses on the chariot trump card have always
been depicted, by either a choice of colors or shading,
as oppositional in character. But this is a small point, for
the real coincidence lies in the fact that this card is preceded by a card called the lovers. The topic of Plato's
analogy—the oppositional qualities of the human soul—
is fitting to the considerations of such occult and mystical systems. In addition the concept of the soul as a
triad composed of a higher quality standing above the
lower two qualities is an idea common to Jewish mysticism. The higher element, the *Neshamah,* is thought of
as the rational element; the *Ruah* is the seat of morality
and ethics, whereas its counterpart, the *Nefesh,* is identified as the grossest portion of spirit, in total rapport
with the body and its instinctual desires. These two latter aspects of the soul could easily be thought to correspond to Plato's two horses, and the *Neshamah* with the
charioteer.

Our earlier discussion of trump card 21 and its possible relation to trump card 1 brought up the subject of
Ezekiel's vision. The central topic of that vision was
God's throne-chariot, *Merkabah* in Hebrew. The image
of the *Merkabah* became a topic of interest to early
Christian writers. In early Christian commentaries this
symbol came to incorporate various symbols and ideas
of Greek philosophy, Plato's in particular. That the Jews
also incorporated the symbolism employed in Greek phi-

---

[7] *The Works of Plato,* ed. by Irwin Edman (New York: Modern
Library, 1928), pp. 286 and 295.

losophy in their thought was inevitable. (The Hellen-ization of the Jews, particularly those located in the famous city of Alexandria, was so complete that they forgot their native Hebrew and had to have produced for them a Greek translation of their sacred writings, the so-called Septuagint.) They are even known to have employed the symbolism of Helios in his sun-chariot in their synagogues:

> Thus, at Beth Alpha, Helios in his chariot drawn by four horses abreast is surrounded by the signs of the Zodiac and of the seasons. The same is found at Naaran and Isfija. . . . Goodenough considers that they have a mystical and eschatological significance, as symbolical of the soul's ascent to God.[8]

It is therefore not unlikely that the Jews might also have borrowed this image from Plato's *Phaedrus* to symbolize their concept of the soul. In fact, one of the most famous Jewish philosophers of the period, Philo of Alexandria, often refers his readers to this particular work of Plato's in his treatises.

One last point to be considered about trump card 7 is the curious canopy over the charioteer. If this card is truly an analogy of the triadic division of the soul, then it too may be a Jewish invention. The previous card—the lovers—actually portrays a marriage scene. The appearance of Cupid above the figures is significant in that this winged figure "was indeed a figure of importance to the Jews"[9] and was employed by them in great profusion.

---

[8] Danielou, *Primitive Christian Symbols*, p. 85.
[9] Erwin R. Goodenough, *Jewish Symbols in the Greco-Roman Period* (New York: Pantheon, 1958), Vol. VIII, p. 5.

Danielou tells us that to Philo,

> the man who would start the mystic struggle would
> be met by a miraculous gift from God, divine eros,
> a gift for which Philo was quite as content to use
> the literary turns and figures of the Greeks as the
> sculptors to use the cupid and other love symbols in
> Jewish art.[10]

Following our line of reasoning, therefore, we might
find in the charioteer's canopy the *huppah* ("canopy")
beneath which Jewish marriages took place. This card
and the one preceding it may simply be paradigmatic of
the marriage of the dissident elements of one's soul by
God.

It is impossible for us to pursue this line of conjecture
further without falling into a long discussion on the nature of Jewish mysticism during the Alexandrian period.
At most, an attempt has been made to present the bare
outline of a suggestion based on what appears to be
more than a striking coincidence.

On the whole we know as little about the true meaning of the tarot as we did three centuries ago. Until the
source of the major trumps is deciphered people will
continue projecting their own beliefs onto their hidden
meaning. Because of the complexity of the symbols,
most occultists have preferred to direct their attention to
the minor trumps, the numerical sequence in
particular. [11] With the exception of the *I Ching* (al-

---

[10] Danielou, *Primitive Christian Symbols*, p. 15.
[11] Almost without exception such considerations involve themselves with the Kabbalistic overlay of the tarot. The reader is directed to Appendix C for a brief survey.

though Aleister Crowley did attempt to include its symbols in his system) practically the whole of Western occultism has at some time or another been included in the tarot system. Astrology especially has figured heavily, each card being assigned to 1 degree of the zodiac.

If nothing else, it may be seen from this brief discussion of four major trump cards the degree to which they elicit conjecture. Our analysis of the possible sources of the figures appearing on these cards may reveal nothing more than the manner in which the mind seeks to discover order in disorder or at least in what is unknown. For the same reason, it would be difficult to believe that the creators of the major trumps did not themselves seek to present the world with an orderly sequence of ideas in symbolic form.

In the tarot we find an amalgamation of the Western occult tradition in new and as yet seemingly incomplete combinations. More than any other of the occult arts, the tarot is used as a fortune-telling device that concentrates on little more than the parameters of one's movement through physical and social space, and ultimately all of the metaphysical statements made within the context of a reading are directed toward the particulars of an immediate future and reality. The contrast between this type of inquiry and that employed by the other arts we have discussed is marked. Astrology primarily concentrates on the psychological profile of the individual, while the *I Ching*'s mode of expression demands that the individual also give attention to influences operating at the cosmic scale. Because it is understood that one shares the activities and operations of the opposites with the universe, that one is intimately connected as it were with the cosmos, the individual is again forced into perceiving the nature of his own interiority.

Kabbalism, which is ultimately devoid of prognostication techniques in any form, solely deals with the metaphysical adjustments an individual must make between himself and the operations of God as displayed in the *Sefiroth*. Again, as in the *I Ching*, there is a concern with the alignment of the personality with cosmic principles. With the *I Ching*, however, the most pressing issue is alignment with the powers of the universe for the purpose of relatedness at either the personal or societal level. One is constantly reminded that the goal is the establishment of superiority of being, of humanity or *jen*.

The tarot, does not concern itself with the psychological limits or potential of an individual as does astrology, nor the ethical dimension that is part of the *I Ching*. It simply deals with the conscious needs of the individual at any given time. Interestingly enough, in those rare instances when it does address itself to the relation between being and God, the tarot employs the symbolism of Kabbalism.

The ideas of unity, duality, triplicity, and quadruplicity that are reiterated time and again in each of these systems might be more than either a metaphysical or symbolic statement, might indeed be a revelation of another dimension without which our immediate reality could not exist.

That the tarot's metaphysical shape began to take on a cohesive and recognizable form only during the latter portion of the eighteenth century may be significant when it is remembered that both psychology and parapsychology came into existence as disciplines in or about the same period. It remains to date the *last* and newest of the occult arts. In the final analysis perhaps the reason that it is so incomplete in itself as an occult art is that it is symbolic of a breakdown. This breakdown involved a shift in focus from a concern with the effect that the transpersonal was believed to have on the world to a scientific investigation of the unknown as it exists *in* the world. What the tarot would therefore represent would be the remnants of the metaphysical cocoon out of which a new expression of the ordering principle emerged in the form of scientific awareness.

5

The Chemical Illusion

The power of God is the worship He inspires. That religion is strong which in its ritual and its modes of thought evokes an apprehension of the commanding vision. The worship of God is not a rule of safety—it is an adventure of the spirit, a flight after the unattainable.

—Alfred North Whitehead

THE FOUNDATION of all alchemic thought was the idea that metals grew in the earth and if left long enough in their dark womb would eventually ripen into gold. Included in this idea was yet another—that of the presence of a spirit in matter as the motivating principle behind this evolutionary process. In time, it was believed, all things would reach their perfection, for this ripening was a phenomenon of the animal and vegetable kingdom as well. Then God's purpose would be fully realized and the divine kingdom would be upon us.

The alchemist sought to speed up this process of nature by imitating her methods in his laboratory. The initial problem was one of discovering the prime matter (*prima materia*) from which the world had been created so that he could release its active agent—the spirit —for the purpose of speedier transmutations. Because it was understood by the alchemist that the perfect metal of nature, gold, could not be duplicated, it was also understood that a philosophic gold need be created for the reception and containment of this released spirit. That accomplished, the alchemist would then be capable of "projections," of effecting further transmutations through the agency of this philosophic gold, or philosopher's stone.

This feat was only to be accomplished by a religious imitation of nature:

> Therefore you must be single-minded in the work of nature, and you must not try now this, now that, because our art is not perfected in the multiplicity of things. For however much its names may differ, yet it is ever one thing alone, and from the same thing.[1]

This is an important point, for it contradicts the general assumption that all alchemists strove to make gold, physical gold, for other than altruistic purposes. When one reads the texts of those alchemists truly concerned with the problem of releasing what they believed to be the imprisoned spirit of God in matter, one is confronted with a seriousness and integrity equal to any scientific inquiry into the nature of man and the universe.

> Therefore all those who desire to attain the blessing of this art should apply themselves to study. Should gather the truth from the books and not from invented fables and untruthful works. There is no way by which this art can be truly found although men meet with many deceptions, except by com-

[1] "Rosarium Philosophorum," in *Artis Auriferae* (Basel, 1593).

pleting their studies and understanding the words
of the Philosophers.[2]

Also to be found throughout the works of the alchemists is the admonition that one must first attain certain
moral prerequisites before he can begin this sacred
work:

For here appeareth what men may it reach:
That is to remember only the true,
And he that is constant in mind to pursue,
And is not Ambitious, to borrow hath no need,
And can be Patient, not hasty for to speed;
And that in God he set fully his trust,
And that in Cunning be fixed all his lust;
And will all this he lead a rightfull life,
Falsehood subduing, support no sinful strife:
Such Men be apt this Science to attain.[3]

The true secret of alchemy was sometimes revealed
by the alchemists to be a spiritual work involving the
transmutation of man himself, the "cleansing" of his own
impurities so that the *prima materia* of his soul might
realize spiritual reunion with God:

And as man is composed of the four elements, so
also the "stone," and so it arises from man, and thou
art its minerals, that is, by the "work"; and it is extracted from thee, that is, by the science. . . .
It is the four elements of the stone, as evenly balanced as possible, which constitute the Philosophical Man, that is the perfect elixir. The stone is

[2] Richardus Anglicus "Correctorium Alchymiae," in *Theatrum Chemicum* (Ursel, 1602), Vol. II, p. 444.
[3] Tromas Norton, "The Ordinall of Alchemy," in *Theatrum Chemicum Britannicum*, ed. by Elias Ashmole (London, 1652), p. 23.

called Man, because it is only through human knowledge and reason that one can reach it. Our body is our stone.[4]

What we are witness to in alchemy is the transformation of philosophic ideas centering about the structure and dynamics of the world into psychological considerations on the nature of man and his soul. The original concern over the nature and mystery of matter here becomes a concern with the "philosophic" nature of the elements that compose matter as they exist in man, a concern that first appears in astrology, which describes the elements as expressive of different personality types. Behind all of this is the idea that there was an original matter, a *prima materia,* which resides not only at the base of the four elements that constitute the world but at the base of our psyches. To understand the significance of this idea to the alchemists we will first have to consider the origin of the prime-matter concept.

The Prime Matter of Alchemy

The problem of prime matter in Western thought originated with the pre-Socratics and culminated in the appearance of Aristotle, upon whose theory the whole of alchemic thought and science came to rest until the early eighteenth century.

According to Aristotle there existed before the creation of the world a chaotic prime substance that only gained existence when given a form. By form Aristotle did not mean only the outline of an object but the specific qualities of the object itself. The qualities were de-

[4] "Rosinus ad Sarratantam," in *Artis Auriferate,* Vol. II, p. 311.

fined in terms of warmth or heat, coldness, dryness, and moistness. These four qualities were then broken down into two sets of opposites: heat-coldness, dryness-moistness. The combination of each of these gave birth to the four elements:

Fire is composed of the qualities dryness and heat.

Water is composed of the qualities moistness and coldness.

Air is composed of the qualities heat and moistness.

Earth is composed of the qualities dryness and coldness.

Each element in this system is thought to contain two qualities, one of which is dominant. In earth, the quality of dryness predominates over coldness; in water, moistness over coldness; and so on. In addition to this, Aristotle proposed that every existing thing is composed of the four elements in union. If you burn a piece of green wood, you will find bubbles forming on its surface (water); the smoke it sends up is the element air; the fire that consumes it is actually being released from the substance itself; and the ash that is left behind is the element earth. Any element may therefore be changed into another element by substituting one quality for another. For example, according to the Aristotelian view water is composed of the qualities moistness and coldness. To change this element into air (vapor) all one need do is substitute the quality coldness with heat.

To the alchemists, and for that matter the whole of Western science, there was no reason to believe that a transmutation of substances could not be achieved given the proper working conditions. The problem was simply one of ridding an element of one quality and substituting another. In alchemy this altering of a metal's form was symbolized by such images as "torturing," "killing," "separating," and all other images symbolic of death. If one could reduce a metal far enough, one would gain *prima materia.*

This achieved, the alchemist would have the seed of things that would then have to be treated in much the same manner mother earth cradled the elements, in a warm vessel. This vessel would be the womb where the resurrection of the thing that had been killed would eventually take place. The important thing was to separate the four elements from each other and from the material worked on, then to reduce each other and from the material worked on, then to reduce each element down to each predominating quality, and finally to re-unite the four primary qualities so that they would form the chaotic state of the first matter. This then became the fructifying waters—to some alchemists the original waters of Genesis before the separation performed by the Spirit hovering over the waters.

When we stop to consider that man was also composed of the four elements in combination, and that these four elements already symbolized four different types of personality or psychological temperament in astrology, we enter into the beginnings of a primitive and intuitive psychology. One cannot fail to find verification of this idea in the following:

> Within the human body there is hidden a certain metaphysical substance, known to only the very few, whose essence is to need no medicament, for it is itself uncorrupted medicament. . . . There is in natural things a certain truth which cannot be seen with the outward eye, but is perceived by the mind

alone. . . . The philosophers have known it, and they have found that its power is so great as to work miracles. In this lies the whole art of freeing the spirit from its fetters, in the same way that, as we have said, the mind can be freed from the body. As faith works miracles in many, so this power . . . brings them about in matter. This truth is the highest power and an impregnable fortress wherein the philosopher's stone lies safeguarded.[5]

The curious statement that the materials are of such a nature that they "cannot be touched by the hands," i.e., are insubstantial, only punctuate Dorn's observation. Here, obviously, we are faced with a metaphysical process—a Yoga of sorts. This further substantiated by the fact that the alchemists identified their "metals" with the planets of astrology, which is to say with "powers":

gold = sun	lead = Saturn
silver = moon	iron = Mars
copper = Venus	tin = Jupiter
mercury = Mercury	

True, a great many alchemists actually worked in the laboratory with actual substances. But they understood that what they were working with was not so much actual substances as spiritual properties concealed in the metals.

The prime matter the alchemists sought was actually a metaphysical substance that was believed to exist not

[5] Alfred Dorn, quoted in *The Collected Works of C. G. Jung*, ed. by G. Adler, M. Fordham, H. Read, and W. McGuire, trans. by R. F. C. Hull, Vol. XII: *Psychology and Alchemy* (London: Routledge & Kegan Paul, 1953), p. 256.

only in the world, hidden and trapped in matter, but in man himself by virtue of the fact that he too was composed of the four elements. This was the true secret of alchemy: By freeing and purifying the spirit in himself, the alchemist caused a reciprocal event to occur in nature—"as above, so below." But this could not be done without the creation of that which was born from the *prima materia,* the philosopher's stone.

The Philosopher's Stone

As mysterious as the *prima materia* is, the philosopher's stone is doubly so. The alchemist's entire purpose was the creation of an incorruptible substance that was believed to be capable not only of bringing other things to perfection but also of healing. The alchemist Hortulanus tells us:

> Hence the parts of the world are infinite, all of which the philosopher divides into three parts, namely mineral, vegetable, animal. . . . And therefore he claims to have the three parts of the philosophy of the whole world, which parts are contained in the single stone, namely the Mercurius of the Philosophers. . . . And this stone is called perfect because it has in itself the nature of mineral, vegetable and animal. For the stone is triple and one, having four natures.

The stone, according to this passage, is the spiritual agency Mercurius, whose activity in the three worlds is promoted and expressed through the agency of the four elements. That is, it is a substance that contains within it, in a unified state, the four qualities of Aristotle. To all appearances it answers the description of the *prima materia*, with but one exception: In contrast to the *prima materia*'s state of chaos the stone is perfect.

A closer glimpse of what this mysterious substance might be is given us in a paper entitled "A Brief Guide to the Celestial Ruby":

> Know, then, that it is called a stone, not only because it is like a stone, but only because, by virtue of its fixed nature, it resists the action of fire as successfully as any stone. In species it is gold, more pure than the purest. . . . It is justly called the Father of all miracles, containing as it does all the elements in such a way that none predominates, but all form a certain fifth essence; it is thus well called our gentle metallic fire.[6]

Turning back to Aristotle, we discover that he too speaks of a fifth "essence," that which "we are accustomed to call fire, though it is not really a fire."[7] The fifth element Aristotle speaks of not only constitutes the planets and the stars but also contains them. This material exists at the outermost reaches of the universe and is called by him the celestial or heavenly sphere. The title of the paper from which the preceding excerpt was taken alludes to this, for as Aristotle adds, "this primary substance and the bodies set in it . . . move in a circle set on fire . . ." thus calling up in the alchemist's mind the image of a "ruby"-colored sphere.

In addition to this the layer immediately beneath the celestial heaven is composed of the element fire itself. Immediately beneath this layer we find the element air.

[6] *Hermetic Museum*, Vol. II, p. 249.

[7] Aristotle, *Meteorologica* (London: Loeb Classical Library, 1952), I, iii, 340b.

These two regions, we are told, come into existence through the action of the sun on the earth: Wherever its rays touch earth, a hot and dry exhalation rises up to form the fire layer; wherever its rays touch water, a cool and moist exhalation rises to form the air layer. The dry exhalation or vapor was later called sulfur by alchemists; the moist, mercury. These two elements were thought of as composing all metals.

As they rise up out of the earth, these exhalations coalesce into minerals, stones, and metals. The dry exhalation forms "all kinds of stones that are infusible—realger, ochre, ruddle, sulpher . . ."; the moist, "iron, gold, copper," which are in a sense,

> water and in another sense not: it was possible for their material to turn into water, but it can no longer do so, nor are they, like tastes, the result of some change of quality in water that has already formed. For this is not the way in which copper or gold is produced, but each is the result of the solidification of the exhalation before it turns to water. So all metals are affected by fire and contain earth, for they contain dry exhalation. The only exception is gold, which is not affected by fire.[8]

Clearly it is Aristotle's fifth element, the quintessence, that is the philosopher's stone: "There is one element from which the natural bodies in circular motion is made up."[9]

And it is this one element that is the efficient cause of everything that transpires in the terrestial region where the elements have their dominion. The trick was to

[8] *Ibid.*, III, vi, 378b.
[9] *Ibid.*, I, ii, 339a.

bring this mysterious fifth pneumatic element down into the terrestial region where it could then mingle with the pneumatic activity of that region. But what exactly is this fifth element? According to Paracelsus, "The prime matter of the world was the Fiat," that is, the Word, the pneumatic Logos, the Spirit of God.

> But such medium they suppose to be the Spirit or Soul of the World, i.e., what we call Fifth Essence, because it consists not of the four elements, but is a certain fifth one, above and beside them. . . . God and Man cannot be united except through a Medium, our Saviour Christ, participating in the two natures, Celestial and Terrestial, Divine and Human.[10]

It was as simple a secret as that. The alchemic work was a religious application of philosophy to nature. The work performed in the laboratory was in every sense a religious ritual in which the attempt was made to ennoble matter with the influx of spirit. One should not find in this idea anything bizarre, for it is the very same intention to be found behind the treatment of bread and wine at Mass. As the "Liber Platonis Quartorum" put it: "Know that the goal of the science of the Ancients is that from which all things proceed—the invisible and immobile God, whose Will brings into being the Intelligence." [11]

The philosopher's stone was more than likely a term for an ecstatic and parapsychological state of experi-

[10] Benedictus Figulus, *A Golden and Blessed Casket of Nature's Marvels* (London: James Elliott & Co., 1893), p. 149.
[11] "Liber Platonis Quartorum," in *Theatrum Chemicum,* Vol. II, p. 119.

ence, one in which the field of immediate knowledge we spoke of earlier became manifest in the psyche of the alchemist. That is, it more than likely answered in many respects the satori experience of the Zen Buddhist. In the opening passages of "The Poimandres of Hermes Trismegistus" we find the writer in the presence of a voice-filled light that tells him:

> That Light . . . is I, even Mind, the first God, who was before the watery substance, which appeared out of the darkness: and the Word which came forth from the Light is son of God. . . . Learn my meaning by looking at what you yourself have in you: for in you too, the word is son, and the mind is father of the word. They are not separate one from the other: for life is the union of word and mind.[12]

A few passages later this voice informs us that God, through the agency of His power Aeon, created the cosmos, and that it is the manifestation of this Aeon in the world that "imposes order on matter," [13] adding a few passages later the idea that "Mind . . . is the very substance of God." [14]

Whereas in all the other occult systems this ordering principle is described as containing the opposites in itself as a principle to be found in the universe, this Greek text frankly states that this principle, or stone as the alchemists called it, should become a conscious addition to man himself:

[12] *Corpus Hermeticum*, ed. and trans. by Walter Scott, Vol. I (Oxford, England: Clarendon Press, 1924), pp. 116–117.

[13] *Ibid.*, p. 209.

[14] *Ibid.*, p. 223.

If then you do not make yourself equal to God, you cannot apprehend God; For like is known by like. Leap clear of all that is corporeal, and make yourself grow to a like expanse with that greatness which is beyond all measure; rise above all time, and become eternal . . . deem that you too are immortal, and that you are able to grasp all things in your thought . . . find your home in the haunts of every living creature; make yourself higher than all heights, and lower than all depths; bring together in yourself all opposites of quality, heat and cold, dryness and fluidity; think that you are everywhere at once, on land, at sea, in heaven; think that you are not yet begotten, that you are in the womb, and that you are young, that you are old, that you have died, that you are in the world beyond the grave.[15]

This passage describes the primal unity suggested as being at the base of the universe, and of the philosopher's stone as well.

I have sought; I have found; I have often purified; and I have joined together; I have matured it; Then the golden tincture has followed, which is called the Centre of Nature (hence so many opinions, so many books, so many parables). It is the Remedy, I openly declare it, for all metals, and for all sick persons. The solution is of God.[16]

These passages from antiquity, especially those from the *Corpus Hermeticum,* remind one of the many psychedelic experiences of the twentieth century. A particularly striking instance is to be found in a work by Masters and Houston:

[15] *Ibid.,* p. 221.
[16] Henry Madathanas, "The Golden Age Restored," *Hermetic Museum,* Vol. I, p. 55.

The surface of my mind, upon which I evolved to a superconsciousness—looked downward, was revealed as a vast illuminated screen of dimensions impossible to calculate. . . . From above, with absolute concentration, observing and sustaining all of this, I was—directing everything, controlling the internal events. . . . The light that illumined these images grew brighter and brighter until I was almost frightened by the intensity of the brillance. . . . I knew that for all its wondrous precision this man-mind even in ultimate fulfillment of all its potentials could never be more than the feeblest reflection of the God-Mind in the image of which the man-mind had been so miraculously created. . . . I opened . . . [my eyes] upon a room in which it seemed to me that each object had somehow been touched by God's sublime Presence.[17]

The point to be emphasized is that the transcendant experience of the alchemists was not drug-induced but was instead the end result of an intricate process of introspection akin to that found in certain Yogic practice. That the West once knew this method in alchemy is a fact we should no longer ignore.

The Stages of the Alchemic Work

Authors differ on the number of stages to be had in the work. Some tell us that there are twelve stages, each aligned with the houses of the astrological archetype. Hence we have the famous George Ripley telling us that the stone is the archetype itself:

[17] R. E. L. Masters and Jean Houston, *The Varieties of Psychedelic Experience* (New York: Dell Publishing Co., 1966), pp. 263–264.

We have an Heaven incorruptible of the Quintessence Ornate with Elements, Signs, Planets, and Stars bright, Which moisteth our Earth by Subtile influence: And ought thereof a Secret Sulpher hid from sight, It setteth by virtue of his attractive might; Like as the Bee fetcheth Honey out of the Flower.[18]

Clearly, the alignment of the alchemic stages with the archetype suggests that the alchemist was attempting to align the particulars of his chart with the archetype that in his mind represented the quintessence or philosopher's stone. He believed that to inculcate order in the world, in the matter, he would first have to bring order into himself. A story told by Richard Wilhelm, the translator of the *I Ching*, touching on this idea, should be of some interest:

Wilhelm tells us that he was once in a small Chinese village that had been for several months experiencing a severe drought. Having tried every available piece of sympathetic magic available to them, the town council finally decided to call in a professional rainmaker. Shortly thereafter, a Taoist monk arrived who calmly asked that he be lent a small room or house at the end of the town where he could withdraw and not be interrupted for three days. On the third day rain fell, and the Taoist priest emerged from his room to begin his journey home. Wilhelm, intrigued by the strange turn of events, approached the monk, and as he puts it, in true Western fashion asked how the miracle had been accomplished. The monk explained that it had been quite simple. While in his own hometown, before he was

18 *Theatrum Chemicum Britannicum*, p. 114.

called to produce rain, he had been in Tao. Upon arriving at the rainless village he was out of Tao. He retired into solitude so that he might place himself back in Tao, and once this was accomplished, he explained, it was inevitable that everything about him would also come into Tao.

This essentially was what the alchemist was attempting to do in his laboratory—align himself with the perfect order of the universe and thereby bring everything about him into order. The alchemist who accomplished this *was* the philosopher's stone himself in that he could transmute reality through the agency of his own spirituality or expanded consciousness. The whole secret of this process was contained in the famous "Emerald Tablet of Hermes Trismegistus," first found in the works of one spoken of as the grandfather of Western alchemy— Jabir ibn Hayyan:

1. I speak not of fictitious things, but that which is certain and true.

2. What is below is like that which is above, and what is above is like that which is below, to accomplish the miracles of one thing.

3. And as all things were produced by the one word of one Being, so all things were produced from this one thing by adaptation.

4. Its father is the sun, its mother the moon; the wind carries it in its belly, its nurse is the earth.

5. It is the father of perfection throughout the world.

6. The power is vigorous if it be changed into earth.

7. Separate the earth from the fire, the subtle from the gross acting prudently and with judgment.

8. Ascend with the greatest sagacity from the

earth to heaven, the powers of things superior and things inferior. Thus you will obtain the glory of the whole world, and obscurity will fly far away from you.

9. This has more fortitude than fortitude itself; because it conquers every subtle thing and can penetrate every solid.

10. Thus was the world formed.

11. Hence proceed wonders, which are here established.

12. Therefore I am called Hermes Trismegistos, having three parts of the philosophy of the whole world.

13. That which I had to say concerning the operation of the sun is completed.[19]

The preceding excerpt refers to the operations of a pneumatic principle, the spirit Mercury of the alchemists, and its effect on the world. The objective is to make that which is below as that which is above, to bring the material world into Tao with the heavens or objective psyche. This is accomplished by an "adaptation" to those formal principles residing in the heavens, such as that achieved by the Taoist monk who brought himself into harmony with the Tao in order to effect a natural balance in things.

But the operations of the spirit Mercury if left to its own devices were thought to be in no way dependable. It was necessary for this volatile spirit to be contained and put through a series of processes. These processes in turn yielded identifiable stages known as the nigredo (blackening), albedo (whitening), and rubedo (reddening).

The nigredo was the most frequently discussed stage

[19] Quoted in John Read, *Prelude to Chemistry* (London: G. Bell & Sons, 1961), p. 54.

of the alchemic process. It symbolized the death stage, the time when the matter being worked was "killed," its basic form broken down so that the spirit believed to be contained within it could be set free. This initial stage of the work was the most feared, and the alchemist likened it to a descent into hell, an immersion in the acid of doubts, during which time the practitioner might not only go mad but also commit suicide. We are told time and again that many alchemists did not survive this stage of the work and that, ultimately, no one could be assured safe passage. At most the outcome was left in the hands of God. For that reason the alchemist warned his reader that he should remember prayer was one of the most important ingredients of this procedure. The painful aspects of the nigredo, always described in personal terms, as if to punctuate its psychological nature, became symbolized by dismemberment, torture, calcination, amputation, dissolution by burning waters, decapitation, wounding, flaying, drowning, starvation, separation, and grinding.

The albedo was sometimes referred to as the dawn state, a time of emergence from the darkness of the nigredo. It is spoken of as the time of the washing, the final cleansing of the impurities found in the nigredo. Because the albedo represents the transition from base lead to silver we often find it symbolized by a feminine figure, a personification of either the moon or nature. If nothing else, this transition points to the emergence of a new awareness or consciousness and for this reason is often associated with symbols of rebirth. Intimately connected with this stage are the ideas of washing, cleansing, and purification. Whereas the first stage stood for a moment of spiritual death, the albedo was thought of as a moment of baptism or return from the depths of the ocean. Its association with the dawn led to the idea that the new awareness was as yet a dim perception, that the sun had not yet made an appearance.

It was with the rubedo that the sun was thought to appear at midheaven to represent the emergence of total new awareness. This stage is always marked by symbols of royalty and dominion, signaling the birth of the philosopher's stone. It is in the alchemist's depiction of these three stages that the reality of alchemy as a psychological process becomes apparent.

The starting point of the entire alchemic process was to be had in the conjunction, or union, of opposites.

The Sacred Marriage

Central to the creation of the philosopher's stone was the problem of the opposites whose union or conjunction was considered the dynamic factor of the alchemic process. Those most frequently employed were sun-moon, sulfur-mercury, king-queen, brother-sister, winged-wingless, and Adam-Eve. In their original condition these were thought to be united but unproductive, in a state of mutual and sterile contamination. The first problem was one of "separating and dividing" the two so that they could each be reduced to their original state. It is for this reason that we sometimes find statements to the effect that the philosopher's stone at both the beginning and end of the process is hermaphroditic.

The depiction of this separation is often given in the form of a king and queen lying dead in a coffin. Once purified, it was then thought necessary that these two principles be reunited so that they might bear fruit. The result of this first sacred union was either the two figures in hermaphroditic form again or the birth of a child. Whichever, the fruit of this union then became the object of the nigredo.

In many instances the alchemic process appears to consist of two conjunctions. The first conjunction was symbolized as a union between king and queen; the second between either mother-son or brother-sister. This second union gave birth to Rebis, or the stone in the form of a hermaphrodite.

Everything we have said up to this point might be construed as being just so much metaphysical gibberish. Much of what is written in the alchemic texts smacks of the fantastic, but as we shall see shortly the process is a real one—and it too points to the existence of a natural expression of the psyche in its attempts to reconcile the conflicting elements of which it is composed.

That the alchemists were actually subjecting themselves to a process of psychological transformation, to a natural and innate process of change contained in the psyche of man, was first recognized by Dr. Herbert Silberer and reported in his *Probleme der Mystik und Ihrer Symbolik*. At the conclusion of this brilliant inquiry into the nature of alchemy, Silberer wrote:

> These typical groups of symbols that the mystic . . . produces as a functional expression of his subjective transformation, can be thought of as an educational method applied to arouse the same reactions in other men. In the group of symbols are contained more or less clearly the already mentioned elemen-

tary types as they are common to all men; they strike the same chords in all men. Symbolism is for this very reason the most universal language that can be conceived. It is also the only language that is adapted to the various degrees of intensity as well as to the different levels of the intro-determination of living experience without requiring therefore a different means of expression; for what it contains and works with are the elementary types themselves . . . which . . . represent a permanent element in the stream of change.[20]

What Silberer discovered was that the symbolism of alchemy had an affinity with those "elementary types" discovered in the unconscious by Freud. Jung was later to follow Silberer into the art of alchemy, during which time he too discovered "elementary types" of symbols manifesting themselves in the psyches of his patients. These he came to call archetypes.

Whereas Silberer's brilliant beginning culminated in his suicide shortly afterward, Jung was to continue with his investigation into the nature of the alchemic art until the time of his retirement. His first large work on the subject, *Psychology and Alchemy,* set the stage for his later statements about the nature of the psyche and its relation to the alchemic process:

There is in the analytical process, that is to say in the dialectical discussion between the conscious mind and the unconscious, a development or an advance towards some goal or end the perplexing na-

[20] Herbert Silberer, *Hidden Symbolism of Alchemy and the Occult Arts* (New York: Dover Publications, 1971), pp. 373–374. Reprint ed. of *Probleme der Mystik und Ihrer Symbolik (Problems of Mysticism and Its Symbolism),* Vienna, 1914.

ture of which has engaged my attention for many years . . . there is in the psyche a process that seeks its own goal independently of external factors.[21]

Simply put, Jung was later to postulate a natural, ongoing process in the psyche toward psychological wholeness that he came to call the individuation process. His concern with alchemy grew out of his belief that the processes contained in the symbolic alchemic texts were attempts to present the methods of the individuation process as they were experienced by the alchemists themselves. Were it not for Jung's thorough investigation into the psychology of this science, its mystery might have remained a closed chapter for several more centuries.

One can see the implications of the alchemic process in the experience of a twentieth-century man in the midst of what is now termed a schizophrenic episode. The choice of this material was made on the basis that the symptoms in this case in every respect correspond to those outlined by the alchemists as symptomatic of the nigredo. The following case history is taken from R. D. Laing's *The Divided Self:*

> Peter came to me complaining that there was a constant unpleasant smell coming from him. He could smell it clearly, but he was not too sure whether it was the sort of smell that others could smell. He thought that it came particularly from the lower part of his body, and the genital region. In the fresh air, it was like the smell of burning, but usually it was the smell of something sour, rancid, old, decayed. . . . He could not get away from the

[21] C. G. Jung, *The Collected Works of C. G. Jung*, Vol. XII, pp. 4–5.

smell although he had taken to having several baths a day.[22]

Peter came to Laing in a severe state of anxiety, guilt, and a general feeling of worthlessness. At the end of his meeting with Laing he said, "I've been sort of dead in a way. I cut myself off from other people and became shut up in myself. And I can see that you become dead in a way when you do this."

Peter's complaints and difficulties break down into the following categories:

1. The complaint of odor:
   a. The odor of something rancid, old, decayed.
   b. The odor of something burning.
2. The depression, anxiety, feeling of worthlessness, and the experience of suffering.
3. The feeling of having been dead and confined.
4. The act of compulsive washing.
5. The localization of odors in the genital region.

One of the most important stages of the alchemic stage of death, the nigredo, was the *putrefactio* ("putrefaction"). It was commonly accepted by the alchemists that the body or element being worked upon would have to die and be allowed to putrefy before the work could be truly begun. In the alchemic text entitled *Splendor Solis* we find a plate depicting a man standing over another's dismembered body (see Figure 14). The text accompanying this plate reads: "I have killed thee that thou mayest receive a superabundant life . . . and

22 R. D. Laing, *The Divided Self* (New York: Pantheon Books, 1969), pp. 129 ff.

the body I will bury that it may putrefy, and grow and bear innumerable fruit." This putrefaction was given great prominence by the alchemists, and there are any number of illustrations depicting the meaning and goal of this process. One such plate may be found in a work called "The Practica . . . Concerning the Great Stone of the Ancient Sages," by Basilius Valentinus.[23]

FIGURE 14

[23] *Hermetic Museum,* Vol. I, p. 339.

FIGURE 15

The illustration (see Figure 15) depicts a farmer sowing seed in an enclosed area. Four crows, symbol of the nigredo, follow behind him, and an angel sounding a trumpet walks toward him. In the center of the picture lies a skeleton, his head resting on a sheaf of wheat. Directly in back of it we see an open grave, a man rising from it and giving thanks to heaven. In front of this man, a bundle of growing wheat. In the background to either side of this last figure two archers fire their crossbows at a target located at the end of the field.

The source for this particular picture is the New Testament statement that unless a grain of wheat dies and enters the earth it has no chance of multiplying. In this illustration we find the sower sowing the seeds that must die before they may be reborn in a new form. The intimate connection between the alchemic process and the laws of both nature and an innate psychological process are here referred to by the presence of the sheaf of wheat beneath the skeleton's head. The spiritual death is literally a harvest. It is the cutting down of that which has grown to its fullest potential, thereby guaranteeing that it will not fall into fruitless decay. The culminating rebirth is here symbolized by the trumpeting angel and the man rising up out of his grave.

Another source tells us:

> Without putrefaction you may not expect to reap fruit from your labour.... Unless you see this rotting of thy compound, which is done in a black colour, with a stinking odour and a discontinuity of parts thy labour will be in vain. You cannot expect to have a new form brought in till the old be corrupted and put off.[24]

Splendor Solis tells us:

> When heat operates upon a moist body, then is blackness the first result. For that reason have the old philosophers declared they saw a fog rise . . . and they also saw the impetuosity of the Sea, and the streams over the face of the earth, and how the latter became foul and stinking in the darkness.[25]

Here we are told that one of the first indications of the nigredo is a stinking odor that rises out of that which is old and in the midst of being cast away. This description corresponds to Peter's complaints of a rancid odor of decay about him. As for the odor of things

---

[24] *Theatrum Chemicum*, Vol. I, p. 247.
[25] Solomon Trismosin, *Spendor Solis*, trans. by "J.K." (London: Kegan Paul, Trench, Trubner & Co., 1920), p. 53.

burning, all of the alchemic texts tell us that the operation of putrefacation cannot take place without the application of heat: "The external heat doth sublime the moisture, which again of its own accord returns continually, and doth moisten the earth so long, until by reason of the heat it have drunk up the moisture wholly, and then it dies." [26]

In *Atlanta Fugiens* we find an illustration of a king locked up in a sweatbox, a fire raging beneath it (see Figure 16).[27] We will have something to say about this

FIGURE 16

[26] *Theatrum Chemicum*, Vol. I, p. 69.
[27] Michael Mair, *Atlanta Fugiens* (Oppenheim, 1618), emblem XXVIII.

symbolism when we get to the symptom of obsessive washing of which Peter spoke. For now it is sufficient to mention that the early stage of the nigredo is always accompanied by the odor of fire and smoke. The heat accompanying this event stems from the emotional involvement the worker finds himself in at this stage—an emotional involvement wavering between terrifying fear on the one hand and impassioned and furious attempts to release himself from his living hell on the other. This brings us to the second of Peter's complaints: depression, anxiety, a feeling of worthlessness, and the experience of suffering.

Chapter VI of the *Aurora Consurgens*, attributed to Thomas Aquinas, begins as follows:

> Beholding from afar off I saw a great cloud black over the whole earth, which had absorbed the earth and covered my soul . . . the waters . . . were putrefied and corrupted. . . . I have laboured night by night with crying, my jaws have become hoarse; who is the man that liveth, knowing and understanding delivering my soul from the hand of hell.[28]

Here we have the outcry of an alchemist at the peak of his suffering. The passage is a statement of utter hopelessness and failure. It is important to point out that regardless of the fact that every alchemist knew what awaited him in the nigredo, there came the time when this initial knowledge faded. No matter how much the alchemist prepared himself, he was inevitably confronted with this moment of truth in which all hope was

[28] *Aurora Consurgens,* trans. and ed. by Marie-Louise von Franz (New York: Pantheon Books, 1966), p. 57.

lost. This preparation for the experience of despair was what the alchemist Michael Maier was thinking of when he wrote:

> There is in our chemistry a certain noble substance over whose beginning affliction rules with vinegar, but over whose end joy rules with mirth. Therefore, I have supposed that the same will happen to me, namely that I shall suffer difficulty, grief, and wariness at first, but in the end shall come to glimpse pleasanter and easier things.[29]

The major difference between the alchemist's experience of the nigredo and Peter's complaints lies in the fact that the former's was induced and therefore psychologically prepared for, whereas Peter's was an involuntary descent into hell without warning.

An interesting aside, which points not only to the universality of the nigredo experience but also to the implication that the alchemist was aware of his own position during the process, is to be found in the following extract from a Chinese alchemic text. Here we are told that if the process is not properly attended to,

> disaster will come to the black mass, Gases from food consumed will make noises inside the intestines and stomach. . . . Days and nights will be passed without sleep, moon after moon. The body will then be tired out, giving rise to an appearance of insanity. . . . Ghostly things will make their appearance to the operator, etc.[30]

[29] Michael Maier, *Symbola Aureae Mensae Duodecim Nationum*, quoted in *Collected Works of C. G. Jung*, Vol. XII, pp. 260–261.
[30] "An Ancient Chinese Treatise on Alchemy Entitled 'Ts'an T'ung Ch'i,'" *Isis*, Vol. XVIII, No. 2 (1932).

It is important to note here that when the "black mass" goes wrong, the resulting effects are *bodily effects.* In other words the alchemists knew that they were essentially working on psychological or spiritual problems and not just on metals. Whenever, therefore, we find statements that during the process of the nigredo metals experience extreme torture, the reference is actually to the mental anguish and suffering of the alchemist himself. He knows that the substances being worked on are, in the words of another alchemist, "extracted from you, and you are its mineral; in you they find it, and . . . from you they take it." [31] Loneliness happens to be another aspect of their affliction: "Because we hand down the art which we have investigated ourselves, to ourselves alone and no one else." [32]

We can see then that the feeling of anxiety, melancholy, and loneliness that Peter complained of is actually yet another sympton of what is plainly an alchemic or psychological process. His experience of death and of being shut up in himself are also symbols of the nigredo. Throughout the literature of alchemy we find the theme of imprisonment and confinement associated with the initial death stage. The matter or the body must be placed in a hermetically sealed vessel, in a coffin, or in a glass prison beneath the sea. The sweatbox in Figure 16 is an example of the prison that the body must be placed in and from which it is eventually reborn.

Peter's fourth complaint is more symptomatic of the

[31] Morienus Romanus, "Sermo de Transmutatione Metallica," in *Artis Auriferae,* quoted in *Collected Works of C. G. Jung,* Vol. XII, p. 300.
[32] *Theatrum Chemicum,* Vol. II, p. 85.

nigredo than of any other. He became a compulsive
washer in his attempt to rid himself of the foul odor of
the nigredo.

The act of washing in alchemy is always associated
with the experience of death and is sometimes expressed
as a death by drowning, an experience of being swallowed up by the waters of the deep unconscious (see
Figure 17). We find this death-by-drowning motif in
emblem XXXI of *Atlanta Fugiens*.

This theme is most familiar to us in the tale of Jonah
where, after his refusal to journey to Nineveh at the
command of God, he is thrown into the sea by his ship-
mates in an attempt to appease the angry God who has

FIGURE 17

caused a tempest to come upon them. Jonah is immediately swallowed up into the belly of a whale for three days and nights; there we find him making the following speech (Jonah 2:2, 3, 5, 6):

> Out of the belly of hell cried I. . . . For thou hast cast me into the deep, in the midst of the seas; and the floods compassed me about . . . even to the soul. . . . I went down to the bottoms of the mountains; the earth with her bars was about me for ever; yet has thou brought up my life from corruption, O Lord my God.

This casting into the sea, this immersion in water and night sea-journey through hell has been performed so that Jonah, as he admits, might be saved from the very corruption that he was asked to speak against at Nineveh. Thus, his death by water becomes a ritual cleansing. In an apocryphal tale we are given the following additional information: Jonah emerged from the belly of the whale naked and hairless. This came about because of the extreme heat in the whale's belly, the heat of hell and imprisonment.

In *Splendor Solis* we find the picture of a man in a hot bath. The accompanying text reads: "An Ancient Sage who desired to rejuvenate himself was told: he should allow himself to be cut to pieces and decoct to a perfect decoction, and then his limbs would reunite and again be renewed in plenty of strength."

The cleansing properties of these infernal waters is aptly depicted in another plate (see Figure 18) from this same text where we are shown a man, black from his corruption and melancholy, rising up out of a river

FIGURE 18

in which he has been immersed, his left forearm already turning white from the effects of the cleansing waters.

The reference to the cutting of limbs in the preceding excerpt from *Splendor Solis* is yet another symptom of the nigredo. The alchemist implies that one literally has to be broken down so that the different aspects of one's personality may come together to form a new pattern. This is akin to what happens in a schizophrenic adventure. Laing has had considerable insight into the necessity of this nigredo process of dismemberment and breakdown, saying, in effect, that people should be allowed to go out of their minds on their own terms. When this process initiates the breakdown in an artificial setting, however, the personality is not totally left to the mercy of chance. The alchemists intuitively recognized the importance of keeping oneself centered and functioning during such a time.

In alchemy that which breaks down the original constitution of the body or the mind is a burning water— the waters of the unconscious into which the adept consciously and purposely lowers himself. The waters not only wash him, they dissolve him. The obsessive bathing Peter performs is the result of a symbolic event exteriorized. He is literally performing what he should be performing within himself, but he has not the "head" to realize this, for it has been "lost" as it were in the chaos of his schizophrenia. *Splendor Solis* emphasizes the importance of "keeping one's head," that which is symbolic of the total conscious personality, during such a process: "I have killed thee . . . but thy head I will carefully hide, that the world wantons may not find thee."

The king is a recurrent figure in many alchemic texts.

We are told in several works that the nature of the king's illness is that he is no longer fertile, that he is in fact impotent. This condition is important when we remember that the odor Peter experiences is localized in his genitals. Something in his personality that was decreed by nature creative has become sterile, worn-out, decayed, and in need of rejuvenation. Peter's problem appears to have been the transformaton of libido, the spiritualization of an instinct. This identification of the problem, the need to spiritualize the instinct with the genital zone, is not unfamiliar to the alchemists. The picture of Adam dying, pierced by an arrow, his phallus turned into the tree of philosophy (see Figure 19), is symbolic enough. All of which suggests that the psychic creative energy that had at one time been associated with the function of creativity at the biologic or instinctual end of the human spectrum has now taken on the function of spiritual creativity—the generation of creative thoughts, philosophy.

Through this discussion some aspects of the experience of a twentieth-century man have been related to the roots of our alchemic tradition, a tradition that grew out of the spontaneous manifestation of a process of development and transformation inherently contained in the human psyche. Peter's schizophrenic experience would have been interpreted by an alchemist as the nigredo gotten out of hand.

Simply put, the experience of death as an initiatory moment in the process of psychological or spiritual development is one in which the individual is torn apart, broken down, dissolved, so that the basic components of the personality may be rearranged in much the same

FIGURE 19

way that a caterpillar's body is broken down and rearranged within its cocoon to yield a newly formed body
—and along with that body, a new purpose.

Although the symptoms of this experience need not be
as marked as Peter's, the quality of the suffering would
more than likely be the same. The feeling of utter despair, the terror of loneliness, the acid of bitter tears,

torturous self-doubts, the fear of insanity, all are symptomatic of this psychological death so necessary for the transformation of personality. The terror of such intra-psychic events might be reduced considerably if they could be seen against the background of the discoveries made by the alchemists.

6

The Future Is Mind

Mind when it fell was made soul, and soul
in its turn when furnished with virtues will
become mind.

—Origen

WE OPENED this work with the proposal that the occult
arts implied the existence of a principle of order in the
human psyche and that a cursory presentation of the
structures underlying each art would reveal qualities
they each share that are suggestive of their common
psychic origin. That these qualities should differ slightly
from art to art should be no more surprising than the
differences to be found between one human skeletal
frame and another.

As we anticipated, several consistent structural patterns did emerge. The exception to the rule was the
tarot, where we found a mixing of elements from other
occult arts within its fragmented form. Because this art
alone is so incomplete, for reasons we discussed earlier,
we are forced to leave it out of our brief summary. It
should be mentioned, however, that each of the structural elements to be summarized do appear in some
aspect of tarot divination. But in every instance it is borrowed from some other art.

The Concept of a Unified Field

The idea of a unified field within which the dynamic principles of both the universe and the created world are contained in a state of harmony has traditionally been symbolized by the hermaphroditic figure of the *anthropos*. In astrology this figure appears in the astrological archetype, which comprises the twelve signs by which the whole of humanity is identified. In Chinese philosophy, while the concept of the Tao is not presented to us in an anthropomorphic figure, the implication is there: The primary constituents of the Tao are the opposites upon which the whole of creation is patterned, and they constitute the differences between the sexes. In addition each human being is thought to contain the very same opposites that comprise the Tao. That the Tao in later Chinese philosophy is identified with the human psyche is no more unusual than the astrological idea that all twelve of the astrological signs play a role in the personality of the individual.

The Kabbalah is no exception to this pattern with its idea of the En-Sof and the figure of Adam Kadmon. The En-Sof also, properly speaking, is not represented in anthropomorphic form and in almost every particular corresponds to the Tao. Whereas the anthropomorphic aspects of the *I Ching* become manifest in the figures of the trigrams and their bodily attributions, in Kabbalism this symbolism is found in the presentation of each *Sefirah* as an aspect of Adam Kadmon's body, after whom the body of man is thought to be patterned. In alchemy, where the figure of Adam Kadmon does play an important part as a symbol of the *prima materia,* the emphasis is on the construction of a philosophic figure, the philosopher's stone, in which the potency of the Godhead in all of its multiplicity is contained.

The overall picture that these arts give us of a unified field of activity ultimately addresses itself to the idea that there is a form of consciousness or being after which our limited field of consciousness is patterned. This idea is frequently found in those creation myths where a divine being models the shape of the human body after his own. The repetition of this theme in mythology, philosophy, and in the occult, at the very least suggests that there may be more psychological truth or basis for its occurrence throughout not only history but the world.

The Concept of Polarity

With the exception of the tarot, all of the arts we have discussed state that the first act the primal unity performed was the establishment of a universe whose dynamism is dependent upon the interplay of two opposing or polar forces. In astrology these become the masculine and feminine natures of the signs, the natures having their origin in the states of dryness and moistness as exemplified by the sun and the moon. The *I Ching* terms these same qualities the yang and the yin, the light and the dark, the masculine and the feminine. So too, the Kabbalah assigns the origin of the opposites to the two *Sefiroth* Hokhmah and Binah. In alchemy, we find the same powers and potencies identified with the sun and the moon, or gold and silver, whose union is necessary for the creation of the stone.

Significantly, each art presents the opposites not only

as representing the energic and motivating principles of the universe, "the force that drives the green fuse," but also, and even more importantly, as the primary constituents of man. Ultimately the identification of the opposites within the individual is given as representative of the human psyche's primary divisions.

The division of the primal unity, then, into the opposites takes form as energic principles symbolic of both our biologic and psychic condition.

The Triune Manifestation of Power

The next manifestation of the primal unity is expressed in terms of a trinity. In astrology this trinitarian activity is known as the quadruplicities; here we find the twelve signs categorized into three sets of activities: the cardinal, fixed, and mutable. In other words the manifested energy of the *anthropos* is divided into three forms of action. Much the same thing occurs in Chinese philosophy where the Tao manifests itself into three planes of activity—the plane of earth, the plane of man, and the plane of heaven. In addition to this, four of the five Chinese elements rule three months of the calendar year. Because man is himself composed of the elements, he too is affected by the passage of the elements from their seasonal birth to death. In Kabbalism, it will be recalled, the world had its origin in the three elements water, fire, and air in the form of the three mother letters, *aleph, mem,* and *shin.* Again, these three elements are associated with the three parts of the human body: head, chest, and stomach. In alchemy the philosopher's stone is thought of as a composite figure whose dynamic principle, the spirit mercury, ranges over the animal, vegetable, and mineral worlds, which are themselves composed of the four elements.

In all of the systems it will be noted that the triune manifestation of the primal unity is performed through the agency of the elements.

The Quaternal Structure of the Universe

In astrology the four-fold division of the *anthropos* is known as the triplicities, each element acting through three astrological signs and therefore through three months as in the Chinese system discussed above.

In Chinese philosophy the four elements of wood, fire, metal, and water group themselves around the fifth, earth. To the Oriental mind there is nothing that is not composed of these elements.

It is only in later Kabbalism that the fourth element, earth, enters the Kabbalistic schema. However, the quaternal structure was earlier expressed in the four-world system where it symbolized the four stages of the manifestation of both God's name (IHVH) and his thought. Again, these four stages are identified with four parts of the human body. The importance of the four elements in alchemy is apparent from our recent discussion.

In every instance these structural characteristics are on the one hand representative of the *anthropos,* and on the other of man. All of which leads to the occult and philosophic statement that the universe and humanity are one in every respect. Again, the insistence with which this theme is repeated throughout the occult arts can only suggest the existence of a psychic principle that seeks to center and thereby stabilize the many components of an individual's conscious and unconscious spheres.

In the long run, there is nothing unusual about the statements made by the occult arts. They all represent and speak of characteristics of being. Occultism looked at from this point of view may be a very practical system by which an individual may learn to relate to himself and to others. Even if the whole of the occult arts are without either scientific or metaphysical basis, even if they should one day turn out to be nothing more than an illusion without substance, they would still stand as very good examples of psychological aids in that they lend to the individual a focus that he might not normally have. Anything that aids the individual in centering on himself, causing him to consider his frailties and enhance his potentials, cannot be considered useless.

Of course, this might make the occult arts sound like a bit of fancy imagination—and perhaps they are just that. When dealing with the empirically grounded facets of the world modern man tends to think of imagination as a useless adjunct. At most it is something to be employed in those pursuits which could be categorized under the label "aesthetic," for imagination as defined is the mental and interior forming of images that have no external reality. Imagination has come to be regarded by the general public as the tool of the child, artist, and creative housewife. But the true fact of the matter is one that has unfortunately been left to the footnotes of scientific history: Imagination is the key to creative genius. A case in point is the manner in which Professor Albert Einstein worked:

In 1864 James Clark Maxwell in England proposed a series of equations to explain light waves in terms of rapidly moving, oscillating magnetic fields. In his "thought experiment" Einstein imagined himself to be riding through space, so to speak, astride a light wave and looking back at the wave next to him. What he should have seen, according to the Maxwell formulation, was a "spatially oscillating electromagnetic field at rest," he wrote later. Yet, he said, "there seems to be no such thing, whether *on the basis of experience* or according to Maxwell's equations."[1]

I emphasize Einstein's reference to his little bit of active imagination as "experience," and not fantasy, the implication being that he found imagination capable of revealing the nature of phenomena normally inaccessible to empirically observable data. At first sight the quality of this "experiment" borders on the fantastic, the manner in which it was conducted reminding one of methods occultists or mediums would employ. In other words, it contains all the elements the skeptic finds objectionable when confronted with systems that rely on associative rather than logical and rational processes. However, we find Einstein qualifying his method in the following:

> The words of the language, as they are written or spoken, do not seem to play any role in my mechanism of thought. The psychical entities which seem to serve as elements in thought are certain signs and more or less clear images which can be "voluntarily" reproduced or combined. There is, of course, a certain connection between those elements and relevant logical concepts. It is also clear that the desire to arrive finally at logically connected con-

[1] *The New York Times*, March 27, 1972; italics mine.

cepts is the emotional basis of this rather vague play with the above mentioned elements. But taken from a psychological viewpoint, this combinatory play seems to be the essential feature in productive thought—before there is any connection with logical construction in words or other kinds of signs which can be communicated to others. The above mentioned elements are, in my case, of visual and some of muscular type. Conventional words or other signs have to be sought for laboriously only in a secondary stage, when the mentioned associative play is sufficiently established and can be reproduced at will. According to what has been said, the play with the mentioned elements is aimed to be analogous to certain logical connections one is searching for.[2]

Einstein here places emphasis on yet another important quality of imagination—play. To his mind, "the essential feature in productive thought" is a suspension of logical consideration in favor of play.

One can take issue with this on the basis that regardless of Einstein's feelings about the nature of "play," the fact remains that what he speaks of throughout is a *mental* operation in which there exists "a certain connection between those elements and relevant logical concepts." Certainly play to Einstein may have been a type of deductive mental operation that to the average man may be nothing short of hard work. But this objection must stem from the attitude that all "mental" operations are of a rational nature. Our problem then, if we are concerned about substantiating Einstein's use of the

---

[2] Quoted in Jacques Hadamard, *The Psychology of Invention in the Mathematical Field* (New York: Dover Publications, 1954), pp. 142–143.

word "play" in the sense that he intended, is to find another example in which play was not so much a mental
operation as it was an actual freewheeling manipulation
of external reality. We find just such an example in
James Watson's account of the discovery of the structure
of the DNA molecule.

Watson surmised that Linus Pauling's discovery of the
α-helix was a matter of common sense and not complicated mathematical reasoning because it was not arrived
at by staring at X-ray pictures of molecules but rather
by "asking which atoms like to sit next to each other."

> All we had to do was to construct a set of mo-
> lecular models and begin to play—with luck, the
> structure would be a helix. Any other type of configu-
> ration would be much more complicated. Worrying
> about complications before ruling out the possibility
> that the answer was simple would have been
> damned foolishness.[3]

His colleagues received the announcement of this
method with considerable reluctance. They did not feel
that play would yield the answer to the problem. Watson went ahead with his plan and made his monumental
discovery: "In place of pencil and paper, the main
working tools were a set of molecular models superficially resembling the toys of preschool children." [4]

Suffice it to say that there are other examples from
the pens of eminent thinkers supporting the thesis that
the nature of things and the universe invisible to the

---

[3] James D. Watson, *The Double Helix* (New York: Atheneum, 1968), pp. 50–51.
[4] *Ibid.*, p. 50.

senses may be attained through the faculty of imagination. Obviously imagination yields truths that are not at first demonstrable via rational procedures. The reasoning employed in such instances may at first sight appear to be irrational but by dint of the results achieved must be called *suprarational*, beyond reasoning.

The occult arts discussed in this book might just be a product of such imaginative thinking. Imagination may have been the very thing that yielded and still yields statements about the relationship of man to the universe based on the existence of a certain fixed ground of existence beyond the range of our perceptions. At least this was the view of the French philosopher René Descartes, the father of modern rationalism, who received the theory of his synthetic and analytic method in a dream:

> I consider that there are certain primitive ideas in us, which are like the patterns upon which we form all our other knowledge. And there are but very few of these ideas, for after the most general ones of being, number, duration, etc. which agree with everything of which we can conceive . . . we have nothing but the idea of extension.[5]

The occult arts may therefore be revelations of the structure of order inherent in the universe, at the base of both physical and psychological realities. That such data may actually be either contained in or revealed through the medium of the human psyche is a possibility the majority of skeptics would deny. Yet, as we have

[5] Quoted in Marie-Louise von Franz, "The Dream of Descartes," in James Hillman, ed., *Timeless Documents of the Soul* (Evanston, Ill.: Northwestern University Press, 1968), p. 121.

seen, there is a sufficient amount of evidence to indicate that there is some substance to such an idea.

Of special interest to our inquiry is the curious fact that with the inception of the *scientific* inquiry into the theory of the unconscious during the first quarter of the eighteenth century, a concerted attempt to formulate a metaphysic of the occult also began, the focus of attention centering on the tarot. From that time forward until the present the two areas—psychology and the occult—have steadily increased in scope, leaving us today with as many psychologies as there are occult systems. Psychology, strangely enough, has primarily concerned itself with the unconscious as a dark and malefic principle, the storehouse of our evils, our repressions, and our fears. The occult, as this book is witness to, has constantly spoken of this field in positive terms, a dimension bearing positive values.

What we have witnessed in these chapters is the consolidation of unconscious impulses generating from an underlying and generally ignored psychic system that speaks of a principle of order contained within the psyche of man. Whatever conclusions a skeptic might arrive at as to the veracity or validity of these occult sciences, the one thing he would have to admit to is the consistency with which this idea is expressed. He would also agree with our statement that these occult arts are products of the deep unconscious, an agreement I am sure would be based on a deprecatory attitude toward the unconscious. That is, he would base the worthlessness of the occult arts on the fact that they are unconscious products and not the creation of a discriminating intelligence or ego; that they are, in short, exemplary of a primitive or medieval way of thinking best ignored. This is the attitude that leads to such statements as sensitives "are by definition sensitive—more emotional than rational, often unpredictable, sometimes of hysterical disposition." [6] In this regard it is of some interest that Professor Cyril Burt, in his Myers Memorial Lecture, made the following observation:

> A number of investigations have shown that the analytic, intellectual mind of the civilized adult seems peculiarly resistant to all types of paranormal cognition. One of the most recent researches is that of Robert and Henie Brier, who tested several samples of people belonging to a society known as Mensa: here the sole qualification for membership is an IQ within the top two per cent of the population. In all the tests of ESP their average score was significantly *less* than that expected by chance. Incidentally this type of research emphasizes the fact that the absence of successful guesses is not necessarily just a negative result: it is always important to note the occurence of a disproportionate number not only of "psi-hits," but also of "psi-misses." [7]

Most skeptics would find comfort in the fact that the members of the Mensa group scored low on their tests, finding justification in the feeling that "intelligent" people do not have much truck with such ideas. More than anything else, however, these tests reveal the existence of a polarity in the psychic system, one end characterized by a discriminating and reflective ego, the other by an open and unreflective system. In other words, the

---

[6] Arthur Koestler, *The Roots of Coincidence* (New York: Random House, 1972), p. 21.
[7] Cyril Burt, quoted *ibid.*, p. 21 n.

strong tendency to maintain the "integrity" of the ego as an unemotional and reflective entity causes a proportionately higher frequency of psi-misses *below* chance—a phenomenon now recognized by parapsychologists to be as significant as psi-hits above chance.

That the more unreflective and open condition of the unconscious is conducive to parapsychological phenomena was recognized by researchers early in the history of parapsychological research. This observation still stands true today and has become the object of special research in areas where the activity of the unconscious is expected to be more pronounced:

> Many investigators have reported changes in ESP scoring level associated with differences in moods, attitudes, and emotional states, and . . . a number of psychoanalysts . . . have reported striking paranormal experiences in their patients. Therapeutic sessions would seem to be an appropriate milieu for investigating ESP because they provide a patient likely to experience strong and labile emotions and a trained observer ready to note whatever changes may occur.[8]

Unfortunately the emphasis placed on the manifestation of ESP as a phenomenon expressive of an unconscious state led to such insinuations as the one proposed by Koestler, that those who are so receptive are emotionally unstable. As one researcher observed: "The emphasis has always been placed on states of low arousal,

[8] John Hudesman and Gertrude R. Schmeidler, "ESP Scores Following Therapeutic Sessions," *Journal of the American Society for Psychical Research,* Vol. LXV (April, 1971), p. 215.

states which are fragmented or dissociated, and states which are not self-directed." [9]

It is this biased view that has depreciated the value of the exacting research performed by parapsychologists—but this is an issue that must be reserved for a different type of book. What is important for us to know here is that there has been a marked shift from the mere monitoring and recording of such undirected parapsychological phenomena to a purposeful investigation of the same phenomena as the product of a self-directed and controlled program. That is, it is becoming increasingly apparent to investigators that such phenomena do not necessarily have to be accidental and unconscious, the latter term here being used in its pejorative sense.[10]

The contention here is that the occult systems outlined in this book are self-directional systems that are capable of producing, through a deep involvement with abstract ideas and a lowering of the threshold of consciousness, altered states of consciousness of the type present in parapsychological phenomena. Furthermore the systems themselves are the product of attempts on the part of the psyche to formally present aspects of its structural makeup to consciousness. Whether or not such an operation points to the existence of a spiritual dimension and impulse is a value judgment we do not care to tackle. That it does point to the existence of a principle of order underlying the psyche, a principle

[9] Darlis Osis and Edwin Bokert, "ESP and Changed States of Consciousness," *Journal of the American Society for Psychical Research,* Vol. LXV (January, 1971), p. 19.
[10] The reader is referred to the enlightening collection of papers put together by Dr. Charles T. Tart entitled *Altered States of Consciousness* (New York: John Wiley & Sons, 1969).

that has a definite structure and with which the whole of our psychological and biologic constitution may be intimately linked, is a matter that should not be ignored. Nor has it been completely.

As early as 1935 we find H. S. Burr and F. S. C. Northrop proposing the existence of a regulating field in a paper entitled "The Electro-Dynamic Theory of Life." [11] The proposals offered in this seminal paper have been followed up during the past forty years by a number of scientists and have culminated in a work by Dr. Harold Saxton Burr that proves the existence of what Burr calls L-fields, "fields of Life":

> *The pattern or organization of any biological system is established by a complex electro-dynamic field which is in part determined by its atomic physio-chemical components and which in part determines the behaviour and orientation of those components. This field is electrical in the physical sense and by its properties relates the entities of the biological system in a characteristic pattern and is itself, in part, a result of the existence of those entities. It determines and is determined by the components.*[12]

The detailed report of Dr. Burr's research methods and findings substantiates Clyde Backster's theory, derived from his polygraph experiments with plants, that there exists an "energy-field blueprint" around which biologic matter coalesces. Burr's L-fields might be what has been revealed to us in photographs taken by the Kirlian method.

[11] *Quarterly Review of Biology,* Vol. X (1935), pp. 322–333.
[12] Harold Saxton Burr, *Blueprint for Immortality* (London: Neville Spearman, 1972), p. 33; author's italics.

We cannot, however, acknowledge the existence of what we have called the "ordering principle," as seen by various researchers working in different disciplines and in the occult systems we have examined, without first questioning the purpose of such a system.

Whereas the occult sciences discussed earlier appear to be constructs representative of a principle of order that presents itself to us through a vast array of cosmologic ideas, alchemy showed itself to be an art that embodied the very process of this ordering principle. The occult arts have been shown to be revelations of self, blueprints of the larger and common framework within which each of our individual psyches takes shape. The value to be found in them is that they allow us access to this hidden dimension, that they are tools for the difficult and forgotten art of introspection through which each of us can come to learn the nature of our individuality. They offer us the revelation of our uniqueness and in so doing force us to come to terms with ourselves.

In each art we found the statement that there resides at the center of each psychic blueprint a principle of order, an energic principle that not only propels man toward a higher form of consciousness but also holds out to those who are willing to look, the promise of transformation. And to those who would still ask, Transformation of what?, we can now answer, Transformation of all that which impedes the natural expression of our common creativity, all that which now grips the world in turmoil and conflict—transformation of those unwanted portions of ourselves that now constitute the *prima materia* of the world.

Appenòix A

Quadruplicities

The quadruplicities refer us to three modes of action: cardinal, fixed, and mutable. The signs are keyed to these modes in the following manner:

Cardinal	*Fixed*	*Mutable*
Aries	Taurus	Gemini
Cancer	Leo	Virgo
Libra	Scorpio	Sagittarius
Capricorn	Aquarius	Pisces

1. The cardinal signs, Aries, Cancer, Libra, and Capricorn, refer us to the modality of activity or action. The four signs associated with this mode of action are thought of as being the most significant in that they symbolize change in its most apparent mode.

According to traditional astrology, these four signs give to the individual an outer goal-directed quality and are expressive of concentrated and focused energy. The individual whose sun is in any one of these four signs would tend to be more involved with the objective than with the subjective view of things, more concerned with outward expression than with interior and personal dialogues.

2. The fixed signs, Taurus, Leo, Scorpio, and Aquarius, refer us to the modality of fixity. These signs are symbolic of the stasis to be found during midseason, the time when all things are concentrated in themselves.

An individual whose sun is in any one of these signs

would have a tendency to remain within the strictures of convention, neither desiring nor seeking change. The energy that in the cardinal signs was expended, directed outward, is here contained, held in check for the purpose of interior dialogue.

3. The mutable signs, Pisces, Virgo, Gemini, and Sagittarius, refer us to the modality of mutability. Traditionally, these are thought of as weak signs by virtue of the idea that they symbolize the death of the seasons, or that period in nature which is transitional in character, partaking of no specific form.

These four signs symbolize energy that has no specific direction, vacillating between the objective (cardinal) and the subjective (fixed). It is for this reason that they are at times referred to as double-bodied signs in that they appear to partake of the modes of activity symbolized by the signs on either side of them.

It must be noted that the modes of activity outlined above are considered to be tendencies rather than fixed patterns of behavior. Each of these modes can be radically altered by the nature of the planets ultimately associated with them.

Triplicities

The twelve signs are next aligned with the four elements, fire, air, earth, and water, in the following grouping:

Fire	*Earth*	*Air*	*Water*
Aries	Taurus	Gemini	Cancer
Leo	Virgo	Libra	Scorpio
Sagittarius	Capricorn	Aquarius	Pisces

Traditionally this grouping of the triplicities is referred to as the result of the radiation or emanation of the cardinal signs' potencies. That is, each cardinal sign is characterized as having radiated its quality 120 degrees to either side of itself, giving birth to the other two signs that then share in its elemental nature. Simply expressed, the four elements traditionally refer us to four psychological types: Fire represents inspiration or intuition; earth, practicality; air, intellectualism; and water, emotionalism. These elemental qualities when modified or accentuated by the quadruplicities cause the signs to be defined as follows:

	Cardinal	Fixed	Mutable
fire:	Aries	Leo	Sagittarius
earth:	Capricorn	Taurus	Virgo
air:	Libra	Aquarius	Gemini
water:	Cancer	Scorpio	Pisces

In addition to the above significations assigned the astrological signs, each is thought of as either masculine or feminine, extraverted and spontaneous or introverted and passive. The groupings are as follows:

Masculine	Feminine
Aries	Taurus
Gemini	Cancer
Leo	Virgo
Libra	Scorpio
Sagittarius	Capricorn
Aquarius	Pisces

The signs are thought of as latent possibilities, poten-

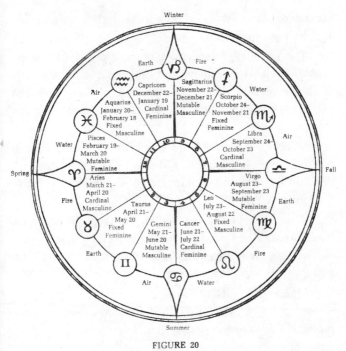

FIGURE 20

THE ASTROLOGICAL SIGNS —
THEIR QUADRUPLICITY, TRIPLICITY, SEX, AND DATES

tialities waiting to be activated by the planets, which are the active and dynamic forces in astrology. Some astrologers believe that the signs and the constellations they stand for represent the body; the moon, the soul; the sun, the spirit; and the five plants—Saturn, Jupiter, Mars, Venus, and Mercury—the senses.

The Planets

☉ The sun represents the masculine principle and expresses itself as vitality and will, the power drive par excellence. It is symbolic of vitality and determination. It rules the sign Leo.

☽ The moon represents the feminine principle and expresses itself as emotional and unconscious influence. It tends to reveal what the individual desires. It is the planet of imagination and fantasy. It rules the sign Cancer.

☿ Mercury represents the intellect shorn of emotionalism. It expresses itself in a desire to interpret, analyze, critically judge, and communicate knowledge. It rules Gemini and Virgo.

♀ Venus represents the ability to love. It expresses itself through aestheticism, pleasure, feeling, and a sense of harmony. It is essentially a gentle planet, knowing no extremes. It rules Taurus and Libra.

♂ Mars represents physical energy. It is a planet of action and expresses itself through impulsiveness, brutality, ruthlessness, courage, and determination. It rules Aries and Scorpio.

♃ Jupiter represents wisdom and understanding. It expresses itself through the agencies of ethics, law, religion, and philosophy. It rules Sagittarius and Pisces.

♄ Saturn represents concentration and inhibition and for this reason is thought to be a planet of restriction or imprisonment. It expresses itself through anxiety and caution and constantly seeks to keep things under control. It is the planet associated with melancholy and death. Its one positive quality is the ability to persevere. It rules Capricorn and Aquarius.

The five planets outlined above are the traditional planets of astrology. The three that follow, Uranus, Neptune, and Pluto, are recent entries, the so-called modern planets. Whereas the traditional planets are sometimes thought by astrologers to contribute the "personal" energies of the personality, those tendencies which would be most accessible to change and modification, the modern planets are thought to project "impersonal" energies, forces residing beyond the personal sphere and therefore least accessible to the personality.

♇ Pluto has corulership over Scorpio and is thought of as an exceedingly powerful planet. Its tendency is to tear things down for purposes either of renovation or of outright destruction. It is also called a higher octave of Mars, meaning that it contains the essence of the energies from which Mars derives its nature.

♅ Uranus has corulership over Aquarius and is the higher octave of Mercury. It is expressive of a cold superintelligence that demands absolute independence, allowing no restrictions of any sort.

♆ Neptune has corulership over Pisces and is the higher octave of Venus. This is the planet of pure fantasy and imagination. It expresses itself through extreme sensitivity, vagueness, and confusion. It is the planet of mysticism.

The Houses

Whereas in the zodiac we are dealing with the division of the heavens, in the house system we are dealing with the earth and the divisions that come about because of the earth's daily rotations, during which time the zodiac makes a complete revolution.

The space surrounding the earth is broken up into four quadrants, each house defining 30 degrees of the horoscope. The lines separating the houses from one another are known as cusps and represent the beginning of a house. The sign found on the cusp of a house determines in what manner the qualities of the house will be experienced.

House	Department of Life
1	personality and identity
2	possessions and money
3	environment and travels
4	the home, past and present
5	children and love
6	work and health
7	the other: marriage and partners
8	death and sexuality
9	religion and philosophy
10	profession and ambition
11	companions and friends
12	limitations and enemies

The fullest understanding of the houses and their relationship to the signs and planets can best be achieved by viewing them in much the same way that one would a sign and its quadruplicity. The first, fifth, and ninth houses, therefore, correspond to the element fire; the second, sixth, and tenth houses, to the element earth; the third, seventh, and eleventh houses to the element air; and the fourth, eighth, and twelfth houses to the element water.

The Aspects

The aspects, a further delineation of the astrological chart, refer to certain angular configurations the planets take up in relation to one another, and the resulting effect. These aspects are broken down into two basic sets: harmonious and disharmonious.

The harmonious aspects are the sectile and trine, 60 degrees and 120 degrees, respectively. The disharmonious aspects are the square and opposition, 90 degrees and 180 degrees, respectively. The last of the major aspects is the conjunction that refers us to planets residing in the same degree, or within *orb*. This term refers to the fact that the angular relationship of any one planet to another need not be *exact;* the two planets under consideration may be in aspect with one another within a certain number of degrees on either side. There are many opinions as to just how much leeway should be given to an orb, but the general consensus appears to be that the orbs for all aspects, with the exception of the sextile, should be 8 degrees. The sextile is allowed an orb of only 6 degrees. The orb is generally thought of as the amount of tolerance allowed for an aspect.

The conjunction presents a special case in that it is considered to be neither good nor bad per se. The conjunction is a convertible aspect, its nature or quality being determined by the planets involved. Therefore a conjunction of Jupiter and Venus, two beneficent planets, is thought of as good; but a conjunction of Mars and Saturn is thought of as being particularly evil.

There are several other factors to be considered when analyzing aspects. The first has to do with the idea that certain planets are not as harmful as others by virtue of their "weight," or mass, which of course has to do with the size of the planet in question. The lightest planet is the moon; the heaviest, Saturn. In order of weight they are: moon, Mercury, Venus, Mars, Jupiter, Saturn.

The strength of an aspect is determined by its exactness, which is in turn determined by its proximity to the exact degree normally assigned it. Therefore, a sextile, whose orb is 6 degrees as mentioned above, is considered to be exact when it is 60 degrees from another planet. This degree is stronger, let us say, than a sextile 66 degrees away from another planet.

The Archetype or Astrological Figure

The archetype, or astrological figure as some astrologers call it, is a diagram of the planets, signs, and houses as they exist in an ideal state, some believing it to be the perfect representation of Adam Kadmon, the world soul we discussed in our chapter on Kabbalism.

It is important for the reader to bear in mind that in prognostication the archetype represents an *ideal* condition, and through it we can determine to what degree any one horoscope deviates. For instance, in the fourth house we find the sign Cancer and the planet the moon. Because the fourth house is defined by the sign of Cancer, the sign of motherhood, the home, and children, it has come to be called the house of the home. The planet that lives there, which is *in domicile* as astrologers refer to it, in addition to being the ruler of the sign residing there, represents the nature of the energy that gives shape to the earthly department the house signifies. Although the signs and the planets have an affinity with the houses, even give them their definition, one must not think that they coincide with them. The fourth house will always be found in the space traditionally assigned it, but the sign Cancer and the planet the moon will *not* always be found there. Thus the archetype is an

aid in identifying the general direction toward which
the individual whose horoscope is under consideration
might work.

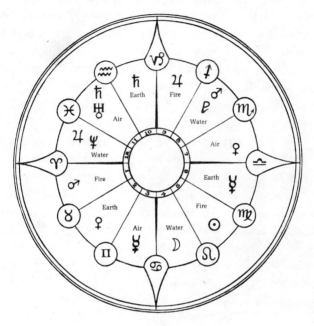

FIGURE 21
THE ARCHETYPE

Appendix B

The Trigrams

The sixty-four hexagrams of the *I Ching* are composi-
ite figures made up of two three-lined figures called trigrams. The reason there are neither more nor less than
sixty-four hexagrams has to do with the fact that there
are only eight trigrams. These eight trigrams combined

one with the other in every possible combination yield sixty-four figures.

The eight trigrams are thought to constitute a family. The father and mother trigrams, Ch'ien and K'un, represent action and quiescence respectively. The sons represent three stages of movement. The first son, Chên, is symbolized by thunder and stands for the beginning of things. The second son, K'an, is represented by water, and stands for danger in movement. The third son, Kên, is symbolized by the mountain and stands for the end of movement.

The three daughters represent three stages of quiescent devotion. The first daughter, Sun, is represented by wind and wood and stands for the gentle and penetrating aspect of devotion. The second daughter, Li, is represented by fire and stands for clarity and adaptability. The third daughter, Tui, is represented by a lake and stands for joyous tranquillity.

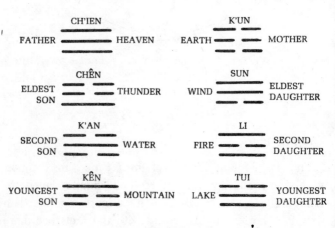

FIGURE 22

There are countless other attributes assigned these trigrams, all of which may be found in the text of the *I Ching* itself, but these are sufficient for proper and general interpretations.

Throwing a Hexagram

The simplest of two methods by which one may obtain a hexagram is known as the coin-oracle method. Taking three coins, the inquirer assigns the numerical value of 2 to one side of the coins, to the "heads" side for example; to the "tails" side he would then assign the numerical value of 3. Throwing the coins he would receive the total value of either 6, 7, 8, or 9:

> three heads equal 6
> two heads and a tail equal 7
> two tails and a head equal 8
> three tails equal 9

Equal numbers are notated by a broken line (— —); odd numbers by an unbroken line (———). Because the lines identified by the numbers 6 and 9 constitute a special case (the *changing lines*), they receive an added notational form:

> ——X—— 6   7 ————
>
> —— —— 8   9 ——O——

Having thrown the three coins once, the inquirer would have received the first and bottom line of his hexagram. For example, throwing two tails and head yields:

> ———   ——— 8

The number yielded by the second throw is placed above the bottom line, and so on until all six lines have been thrown (see Figure 23).

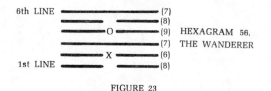

6th LINE ══════════ (7)
       ════ ════ (8)
       ════O════ (9) HEXAGRAM 56,
       ══════════ (7) THE WANDERER
       ════X════ (6)
1st LINE ════ ════ (8)

FIGURE 23

Turning to the hexagram in the *I Ching*, the inquirer will find the textual information up to but not including the heading "the lines." If none of the lines in his hexagram have been given prominence by the numbers 6 or 9, the reading is complete. In our example, however, we have two changing lines, the second line having been formed by a 6, the fourth by a 9. The inquirer would then read the textual information accompanying the second and fourth lines, and then change them into their opposites. The broken line would be changed into an unbroken line, and the unbroken line would be changed into a broken one. This would result in hexagram 18, shown in Figure 24. The inquirer would now be referred to the commentary appended to this changed hexagram.

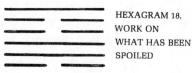

════════ HEXAGRAM 18,
════ ════ WORK ON
════════ WHAT HAS BEEN
════ ════ SPOILED

FIGURE 24

The other method of throwing a hexagram is known as the yarrow-stalk method. Purists insist that this is the only method one should employ. It is a long and complicated procedure, the explanation of which may be found in the Wilhelm-Baynes translation of the *I Ching*.[1]

The Changing Lines

The concept of the changing lines, resulting in a changed hexagram, is related to the idea that the yin and yang lines are each thought of as subject to two states—a state of equilibrium and a peak state, a state of change. A yang line with the numerical value of 7 is thought to reside in a state of equilibrium, as does a yin line with the numerical value of 8. A yang line with the value of 9 and a yin line with the value of 6, however, are representative of transitional stages. That is, both the yin and the yang in these instances are thought to have reached their peak of energic expression. They then fall into a special category answering a law of the opposites: They change into their opposite. Such lines are referred to as "being in motion," or "changing."

Basically, every hexagram is thought of as containing within it six stages of development symbolized by the statements appended to the lines. When one receives a hexagram with a changing or moving line, what is stated is that the time of the hexagram is being more finely delineated. A hexagram received without any changing

[1] *The I Ching or Book of Changes,* the Richard Wilhelm translation, trans. into English by Cary F. Baynes (New York: Pantheon, 1955).

lines points to the idea that one stands before the time as if one stood before a doorway—the time has not yet been entered, any and all possibilities inherent in the combination of changing lines contained within it are still possible.

On the other hand, a hexagram with a changed or changing lines refers us to the idea that the time is already upon one and is no longer a question of possibilities. A hexagram without changing lines should therefore be read in its entirety because each of the six lines is a potential of the time, and by attending to the statements appended to them one might either purposively circumvent or bring to expression those characteristics of the time by giving them due consideration.

In a hexagram containing changing lines the time has already been brought into play. The function of the changing lines is to show the individual the manner in which he has brought this particular time about, and sometimes the prescription. As a rule it is the changed hexagram that gives the prescription. The first hexagram, then, reveals the nature of the time and how it has come to pass. The changed hexagram that follows reveals one of two things: either the solution to the problem or time under consideration, or an amplified vision of it for closer viewing.

The Nuclear Hexagram

A further aspect of a hexagram has to do with one of its major internal components, the nuclear hexagram. The nuclear hexagram is composed of two nuclear trigrams—the second, third, and fourth lines constituting the lower primary trigram of the nuclear hexagram; the third, fourth, and fifth lines constituting its upper primary trigram. In the hexagram shown in Figure 25, hexagram 3, Difficulty at the Beginning, the nuclear hexagram turns out to be hexagram 23, Splitting Apart. The nuclear hexagram is that which gave birth to the hexagram in which it is contained. It is the seed of the past. To show the veracity of this statement we shall take the discussion of the two hexagrams in Figure 25 a few steps further.

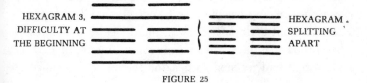

HEXAGRAM 3, DIFFICULTY AT THE BEGINNING

HEXAGRAM . SPLITTING APART

FIGURE 25

One of the attributes of the trigram Kên, the upper primary trigram of the nuclear hexagram, is fruits and their seeds. The text accompanying the sixth line of this hexagram informs us that there is a large fruit still uneaten. This fruit is the topmost line of the Kên trigram. In the hexagram that immediately follows, hexagram 24, Return (Turning Point), we find contained in the image of the hexagram a seedling beneath the earth, the Chên trigram beneath the K'un trigram. This latter hexagram refers us to the idea that the yang force that has been banished during the winter period, pushed out of the picture as it were, the solitary yang line being pushed up and out in the preceding hexagram (23), here returns. What was contained in the fruit of the top line of hexagram 23 becomes reborn.

Hexagram 3 reveals the difficulty of the return. On the one hand we are told that there is an obstacle in the way in the form of a stone (upper nuclear trigram of hexagram 3), but what is implied by this has more to do with the idea of winter at a standstill, as the end of things. The difficulty at the beginning comes about because of a precondition, the stone of winter. What has brought this time about was the past, the time of splitting apart, the death of summer.

Relating this to the practical and mundane sphere rather than to the sphere of natural phenomena, the stone in hexagram 3 may refer the individual to the presence of an obstacle that comes about because of a time of splitting apart. That is, the difficulty under consideration will have had its beginnings in an earlier situation that had reached its peak of possible development.

Appendix C

The Influence of Kabbalism on Tarot

Sometime around the sixteenth century the four suits of the tarot—wands, cups, swords, and pentacles—became identified with fire, water, air, and earth, respectively. These designations were then aligned with the triplicities of astrology. In addition the suits were then caused to correspond with the tetragrammaton, which is in turn symbolic of the four worlds.[1]

Therefore each element was thought of as the product of one of the four worlds. This led to the idea that fire was the first element in the creation, symbolic of the archetypal principle of order as contained in the mind of the En-Sof. Water, the element synonymous with the

[1] See Figure 12, p. 130.

cups suit, would therefore be representative of creative ideas or intuitions. The third element, air, synonymous with the swords suit, is symbolic of the principle of formation or formative thought. The last element, earth, that which is synonymous with the pentacles suit, corresponds to the fourth world known as the world of making, the concretization of reality we call the world.

In addition to the above associations the four court cards, king, queen, prince, and knave, are also symbolic of both the elements and the tetragrammaton. This leaves us with the following table:

fire	wands	kings	I
water	cups	queens	H
air	swords	princes	V
earth	pentacles	knaves	H

The modern occultist understands that the court cards are thought of as having dominion only over the suits aligned with them. That is, keeping in mind that each court card rank is composed of the four suits, in the grouping of the four kings the kind of wands would be truly representative of "kingship," whereas the king of pentacles would be understood to bear a smaller amount of the potency contained in the king of wands. By the same token the knave of pentacles would be that card most representative of earth, and so on.

The Number Cards and the Sefiroth

The sequence 1 (ace) through 10 of each suit is thought to correspond to the arrangement of the *Sefiroth* of Kabbalism.

ace (1)	Kether	6	Tifereth
2	Hokhmah	7	Netsah
3	Binah	8	Hod
4	Hesed	9	Yesod
5	Gevurah	10	Malkuth

The number cards of each suit also break down into properties of the four worlds:

1. *'atsiluth,* the world of emanation = all aces, 2's, and 3's.
2. *beri'ah,* the world of creation = all 4's, 5's, and 6's.
3. *yetsirah,* the world of formation = all 7's, 8's, and 9's.
4. *'asiyah,* the world of making = all 10's.

Another system of correspondences is that given us by Papus in his *Tarot of the Bohemians.*

Papus arranges the tetragrammaton as shown in Figure 26. The first letter of the tetragrammaton, *yod* (I), is explained by Papus to be an active masculine principle. This is immediately followed by the first *he* (H), which he explains as a passive and feminine principle. These two, then, might be referred to as father and mother, which give birth to the *vau* (V), representative of the combined energies of the first two letters in the agency of a son. The second *he* (H) he explains as indicating "the passage of the Trinitarian law into a new application—that is, to speak correctly, a transition from the metaphysical to the physical world, or generally, of any world whatever to the world that immediately follows it." [2]

[2] Papus, *The Tarot of the Bohemians,* trans. by A. P. Morton (New York: Arcanum Books, 1962), p. 22.

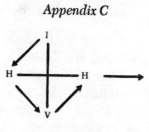

FIGURE 26

He then suggests that the four court cards be aligned with this scheme and explains that we are to continue this application with the ten numbers to arrive at Figure 27.

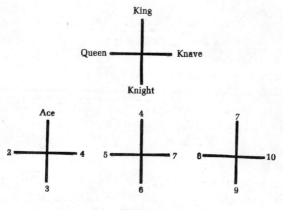

FIGURE 27

From this we derive the following table:

I	kings, aces, 4's, and 7's
H	queens, 2's, 5's, and 8's
V	knights, 3's, 6's, and 9's
H	knaves and 10's

Apparently, by manipulating the tarot cards in any of the above series of correspondences we can bring about further correspondences. From the literature existing on the subject, we find that this is exactly what has been done. Little of what has been written about it, however, tells us more than Kabbalism or astrology already do. Surveying the material and its implications, one gets a sense of frustration, as if something has gone amiss.